Guglielmo D'Izzia's first novel is a dish seasoned with mystery, suspense, sensuality and Sicily. A slow train ride, an unscheduled stop in a southern Italian town inhabited by a collection of unpredictable characters who leap into your imagination with more fervor than the heat and fever of a Sicilian sun. This darkly lit mystery, delivered with quick and natural dialogue, takes many twists and turns leading to the suspense of the very last page. A fine debut from a writer you will hear from again and again. .

—**Gianna Patriarca**, author of *Italian Women and Other Tragedies* and *All My Fallen Angelas*

The Transaction leaves us feeling like Mr. Jones in the Dylan song: something is happening, but we don't know what it is. De Angelis is on a business trip to a small provincial town in Sicily, but his business is soon undone, and we begin to wonder if he'll survive and whether he cares if he does. There's a bit of Camus and a bit of Kafka in this taut novel.

—**Lee Gowan**, author of *The Last Cowboy*

Absurd in all the right ways, *The Transaction* reads almost like what Kafka would have written if he'd been asked to do a remake of Scorsese's *After Hours* but set in Sicily and over the course of a week instead of a night. Its hapless and deceptive (and perhaps above all self-deceptive) narrator is thrown back and forth between situations he claims not to understand, gets into fights he can't remember, and keeps putting his foot into his mouth, but when given the chance to flee he instead wades in deeper. A strange and dynamic and entertaining debut.

—**Brian Evenson**, Guggenheim Fellow and author of *A Collapse of Horses*

the Transaction

Essential Prose Series 174

Guernica Editions Inc. acknowledges the support of the Canada Council
for the Arts and the Ontario Arts Council. The Ontario Arts Council
is an agency of the Government of Ontario.

We acknowledge the financial support of the Government of Canada.

the Transaction

Guglielmo D'Izzia

GUERNICA
EDITIONS
TORONTO · CHICAGO · BUFFALO · LANCASTER (U.K.)
2020

Michael Mirolla, editor
David Moratto, interior and cover design
Dejan Radic, cover image: *Fly and Thistle*
Guernica Editions Inc.
287 Templemead Drive, Hamilton (ON), Canada L8W 2W4
2250 Military Road, Tonawanda, N.Y. 14150-6000 U.S.A.
www.guernicaeditions.com

Distributors:
Independent Publishers Group (IPG)
600 North Pulaski Road, Chicago IL 60624
University of Toronto Press Distribution
5201 Dufferin Street, Toronto (ON), Canada M3H 5T8
Gazelle Book Services, White Cross Mills
High Town, Lancaster LA1 4XS U.K.

First edition.
Printed in Canada.

Legal Deposit—First Quarter
Library of Congress Catalog Card Number: 2019946877
Library and Archives Canada Cataloguing in Publication
Title: The transaction / Guglielmo D'Izzia.
Names: D'Izzia, Guglielmo, author.
Series: Essential prose series ; 174.
Description: First edition. | Series statement: Essential prose series ; 174
Identifiers: Canadiana (print) 20190158514 | Canadiana (ebook)
20190158565 | ISBN 9781771834544 (softcover) |
ISBN 9781771834551 (EPUB) | ISBN 9781771834568 (Kindle)
Classification: LCC PS8607.I98 T73 2020 | DDC C813/.6—dc23

To My Parents

 *Chapter One*

I **must've fallen** asleep. The lady and the two excited kiddies are not here anymore—their luggage, gone. Only breadcrumbs and the pungent, almost nauseating smell of *capuliatu*, as she called it, are left behind. "We're getting off at Messina Centrale," I remember her saying, amid the hurly-burly of the two little monkeys. This must be Sicily, then. I check my pocket watch: two o'clock. The train was supposed to arrive at Malabbina at around one forty-five. I rush to the window looking for a sign of some sort. Not a thing. The train is stopped in the middle of the country-side. Sweeps of yellow scrubland stretch before me with no more than a few isolated houses in the distance to disrupt the monotony of the landscape.

I hasten to the corridor and look into the adjoining compartment. It's as empty as the rest of the coach. I run to the connecting car, but the door is stuck. I try to force it open. Nothing. As I pound on it, a deep raspy voice calls out behind me: "Sir? What're you doing?" The voice belongs to the train conductor, a moon-faced middle-aged man with a ruddy complexion and a massive frame.

"Sorry, I was trying to get to the other coach."

"Is this some kind of joke?"

"Excuse me?"

"That door is locked. This is the last passenger car. Can't you see?"

I stoop slightly and peer through the little window. Nothing but endless tracks, more undergrowth to the right, and down below to the left a flat shimmering sea. I hadn't realized we were so close to the coastline. In the haze of the moment, I ran to the wrong side of the coach. Unable to conjure up a plausible excuse, I smile.

"May I see your ticket, sir?"

"My ticket? Why, yes, of course. It's in my jacket."

Once back in my compartment, I explain to the conductor what happened, not that I have to. I suppose I don't want to pass for a loony. He tells me, candidly but with a hint of a smirk, that extreme heat can make you do bizarre things, especially if you're not used to it. He also reassures me I haven't missed my stop, which is still quite a few kilometres away, although I'll probably miss my connection to Figallia, and adds that due to technical problems we're being delayed. He's quite vague about that, though. In any case, we have a little laugh as he reluctantly makes his way out of the compartment to resume his duties.

Still exhausted from the long trip and with no respite from the sweltering heat, I flump in my seat. Even the cicadas' laments seem to be inveighing against the blistering sun. Amazingly, in spite of their maddening screeching, I go from daydreaming to sleeping without realizing it.

When I wake up, one hour has past, according to my pocket watch. Sweat-sodden, I stick my head out the window, only to discover the train hasn't moved a centimetre. Exasperated, and trying to take my mind off the heat, I decide to take a closer look at the papers before meeting with my contact.

They are in my bag, an old-fashioned hessian suitcase with a brass clasp on either side of the handle. The luggage stares at me mockingly from the rack high above and directly across my seat. I summon the strength to hoist myself up and reach for it. It seems to have become heavier. I lower it to the seat.

There's so much stuff packed in it that as soon as I place my thumbs on the clasps they spring open. I lift a stack of clothes and fetch the folder I compiled, containing the broad strokes of the proposed deal and pretty much all I need to know. Under it, there's a second file, the extended version, so big you could knock someone unconscious with it. I have to use rubber bands to keep it all together. The signature note penned by my boss Montanari is paper-clipped to the top right-hand corner.

It says: *Read me.*

I take that folder out of the luggage as well. Montanari has put literally everything in it. There's also a frontispiece, a sketch of the area, a table of contents, and the whole thing is colour-coded, cross-referenced even. I leaf through the property section, which is fairly straightforward, save for a little contention concerning a small segment of the northeast border and the somewhat woolly details on the vacant warehouse right in the centre of the estate. He's put another little note there:

Talk to the Sinzali (that's sicilian for mediator) about the warehouse, and make sure everything is up to code. His name is Giuseppe Tommasini, or Peppe as the locals call him. He's the one who's arranged everything for your stay as well. I know we discussed this already. But, anyway, he'll pick you up at the train station at Figallia. It's a really tiny place perched somewhere in Palermo's hinterland. By the way, I didn't put a picture of Peppe because I don't have one. From what I gather, he's about 170 centimetres tall, short black hair, not skinny but not fat, average looking. I'm afraid that's all I've got.

Someone yells: "Everybody off the train."

I let go of my papers, which scatter all over the floor, and hurry to the window to see what's going on.

"Everybody off the train," the voice shouts once again.

Blinded by the sun, I can't make out where the voice comes from at first, but as my eyes adjust, I recognize the enormous paunch of the train conductor.

"What's going on?" I ask.

"I'm afraid you're gonna have to get off the train, sir. Bring your luggage with you."

The conductor wipes his brow and neck with a hand towel.

"What do you mean, 'get off the train'?"

"The engine broke down, and there's nothing we can do about it, at least for now. Collect all your stuff. We're gonna walk to the nearest station. There's a whistle-stop a few hundred metres down there, tucked away behind that slope. It's a small one, but that oughta do it."

"Can't we just wait here until they fix it?"

"It's not safe. We're gonna have to move before it gets dark."

I want to ask why, but somehow I fear what he might answer, so I don't say anything. I go back inside and collect my belongings.

* * *

Off the coach, I notice the train has been considerably downsized. What's left are five passenger cars plus the locomotive. I could swear there were more than ten when I boarded almost twenty-four hours ago in Milan. It's hard to imagine I slept through all that. I know the train goes directly into the ferry for the crossing to the island, but the decoupling of the cars at Messina Centrale? I must've been comatose.

"All right, everybody … gather round!" the conductor shouts in a surly tone. He's standing by the locomotive, impatiently gesturing us to join him.

To my surprise, a scattering of people emerges. The train had been as crowded as a cattle car. There's barely a handful now, indolently filing towards the conductor. The others are men, mostly in their forties if I were to guess, clearly southerners, and all, but the two young soldiers carrying absurdly over-sized olive-green-canvas knapsacks, travelling light.

The locomotive provides a little bit of shade, and we're

all trying to squeeze into it. I push my back as close as possible to the car without touching the searing metal carcass. The conductor stands beside me, holding some kind of logbook in his left hand. He's sweating so profusely he has to wipe his brow every other second. He looks at me for a moment, as if proffering an apology for his over-perspiration, then leans to one side. His eyes bounce from passenger to passenger. "Where's the old lady with the funny dog?" he asks, failing to address anyone in particular.

Nobody says anything.

Our eyes meet again. I shake my head. He whisks his eyeballs back to the other passengers. They all appear as though utterly, yet malevolently, oblivious to their surroundings. "The old lady! With the funny dog?" he asks, his voice deafening and pregnant with irritation.

The rest of the passengers finally aim their opaque stares at him, but still not a single one says anything.

"Well?" he says, shattering the fraught silence.

As we all eye each other, the conductor raises his chin, takes a step to the side, away from the locomotive, and glances beyond the last passenger in queue.

We all turn in unison.

From the second coach's door, a segment of a luggage sticks out. It must be the old lady's. Like the conductor, I lean to one side and step away from the locomotive to get a better viewing angle; most of the other travellers echo. The old lady's head, swathed in a black headscarf, protrudes from the coach as if discarnate, her neck preposterously elongated. She quickly moves it around in all directions like a bird and just as quickly withdraws it.

After a spell, the lady's head re-emerges, this time along with the rest of her. She stands there for a second, looking downward—at the flight of steps, I assume. Turning sideways, she attempts to land her right foot on the first step. Something causes her to change her mind, however, for she retracts her foot and withdraws inside the coach—only to come out again, posterior first. Once more, she tries to lower her Rubenesque figure to the ground, her right leg and foot fully extended, reaching for the top step. But the sharp drop and perpendicular position of it leaves her foot stranded and dangling in the air.

"What's the matter with you? All of you ... You should be ashamed of yourselves!" the conductor bellows. "You two"—talking to the off-duty soldiers—"especially. You're a disgrace to the very uniform you're wearing. D'you know that?" The two privates look positively stunned: their eyes gaping, their mouths ridiculously ajar. It takes them more than a moment to fully fathom what the conductor is inferring, judging by the gradual change of their facial expressions, which shift from that of shock, to bitterness, to humiliation. "Can't you see she needs a hand?" The lady is still trying to reach the first step. "What the hell are you looking at? Go help her, for Chrissakes!"

The soldiers unfasten the buckles holding their knapsacks, let the bags drop to the ground, and rush off to help the old lady. After they usher her down the steps, one of them, the slender one, reaches for the luggage still half sticking out of the coach and lowers it to the ground; then, with impressive athleticism, he vaults over the flight of steps and vanishes into the car. He reappears and jumps back down holding in his arms the smallest dog I've ever seen. The old lady rushes to snatch the whimpering creature off the soldier's arms and, without even the least sign of gratitude, walks toward us. The soldiers follow suit.

"Okay, now that we're all here we can get a move on," the conductor says. "I know it's not that long of a walk, but don't you get fooled; this torrid heat can be very dangerous, so if you have any hats or whatever, I'd recommend you put them on." And addressing the cantankerous old lady, he adds: "You let me know if you need anything, anything at all." She grunts something unintelligible and, with a brusque hand gesture, shrugs him off. The conductor's lip curls in a quite visible bout of contempt. "All right, let's get going."

At once, all the men, except the soldiers, who are already wearing their standard black bonnets, reach for their trousers' back-pockets and take out some kind of rolled-up tweed flat caps. They whip them open and put them on. I don't have either a bonnet or a flat cap or any other hat for that matter, so I use the next best thing at hand: a kerchief.

"Follow me," the conductor says and forges on ahead.

For a person his size, and despite his almost dizzying undulating-gait, the conductor moves fast. I'm walking a few strides behind him, trailing in his wake and barely able to keep up with his pace. The old lady is next to me, toiling along, and the two soldiers, carrying her stuff, shadow her. She's holding the panting little creature tight to her bosom; the poor thing is really struggling with this heat: its muzzle, agape; its tongue, hung to the side; its large and protuberant eyes, turbid.

A good stretch of parched terrain already separates

us in front from the rest of the caravan, who saunter along bunched in twos and threes. The conductor halts for a moment and turns around.

"How's everybody doing?" he shouts. "Okay?"

Nobody answers.

"You see that?"—he's pointing at an incline ahead of us—"Well, we're gonna go right around that all the way to the rear, but first we gotta go down this little path here. It's not that steep, but watch your step anyway."

He pulls up his pants and eases himself down the pathway. By the time I stand on the verge of the trail, gazing down at it, the conductor has already reached the flat plane at the bottom and sought shelter under a lone tree. No doubt, the blinding sun and the thick haze can make it difficult to judge distances properly, but the little path, as the conductor called it, is a good deal steeper than he let on. It slants and curves quite sharply; and to complicate things, patches of thistles disseminated throughout the path nearly obstruct it in certain spots.

From under the tree, the conductor gestures to join him. "Don't be afraid! It's not as bad as it looks."

I wave at him and turn around. The old lady is looming merely a foot away from me, staring at the trail, her face crumpled in displeasure. Like bronzes, the soldiers stand a hairbreadth behind her. I step aside and signal to them to go ahead with the lady. They thank me and, as in a synchronized formation, move right ahead in front of her, perhaps so as to create some sort of barricade for her to latch onto as they descend. Before moving, however, the slender one attempts in vain to take the dog off the old lady. They throw a fleeting glance of resignation at each other and, without further vacillation, edge down the path. I follow them.

Almost immediately, it becomes painfully clear I made a mistake. The lady is advancing at an unbearably slow pace, and the sun is beating against the top of my head with such force I can hardly keep my legs from folding down to the ground. I try to pass them, but the path, which is carved into the ground, is so narrow it can't fit more than two people at once.

At last, we arrive at the tree where the conductor is expecting us, but by now I feel so woozy my head is spinning.

"You okay?" the conductor asks.

"Yes ... I'm fine ... "

"You sure? 'Cause you don't look too good."

"I don't know ... I feel ... a bit —"

 *Chapter Two*

"**W**ake up! ... Come on, wake up!"

"*Aviti a pigghiari n'anticchia d'acitu, senti a mia ... e cciu faciti sciavuriari.*"

"*No, no, no, no, ccia njittari nu pocu d'acqua fridda nta frunti!*"

"*U dutturi avemu a mannari a chiamari.*"

"*Ma chi murìu?*"

"*Tutti quanti vatuvinni! ... Forza, scumpariti! Signuruzzu beddu! ... Cci vuliti lassari spazziu ppi respirari?*"

"*Si muvìu. Talè! ... Talè! Talè!*"

The stifled hum of voices subsides, and my eyelids slowly lift, battling some sort of gravitational pull.

"How are you feeling?"

The rotund face of the conductor is staring right at me, his features almost indistinct, his shapeless mouth moving, his voice as if coming through a thick sheet of glass.

"You all right?"

"What happened?" I manage to exhale.

"You fainted. Under the tree. You don't remember?"

"No." I prop myself up a bit. "The last thing I remember is ploughing my way through those goddam thistles. After that ... I don't know ... I do remember the tree though—"

"Well, you seem better now," the conductor says, smiling.

"I'm fine ... I'll be fine, thank you. Look, I'm sorry for ... Hell, I don't even know ... "

"No need to apologize. It happens. What's important is that you're all right now."

As I scan the space—the bare waiting room of a train station with only a few uncomfortable wooden benches and cigarette butts all over the floor, I recognize most of the passengers. Aside from the old lady, who's still cradling the tiny creature, sitting on the bench to my left, adjacent to the one I'm half-lying on, the remainder of the passengers are across from me, either resting on those benches or on their luggage, murmuring in my direction. Maybe it's my imagination, but I have the impression they aren't too fond of me.

"How long was I out?"

"About ten minutes, I'd say. We almost sent for a doctor."

"Where's my luggage?" I ask, lowering my feet to the floor. With an upward tilt of his head, the conductor directs my attention to somewhere behind me. I half turn my neck. The luggage is safely resting by the wall under the large window next to what looks like the main entrance of the station. I turn back, nod in appreciation, and lift myself up. "What now?"

"What do you mean?"

"I mean, how do I continue from here?"

"Let's see ... You were supposed to transfer at Malabbina, am I right? ... Going to Figallia, is it?"

"Yes."

"Well, that's not gonna happen. I'm afraid the last intercity bus has already taken off."

"So, I'm looking at a layover?"

"I'm afraid so."

"I suppose I should find myself a hotel then." Everybody laughs. "What? What did I say?"

His paunch still shaking, he explains we're in a very small village, and the locals have no use for a hotel. According to him, it's a miracle they even have a train station.

"What about the train?" I ask, dreading the idea of spending the night on those benches.

"They're sending a switcher, but that'll take a while. In any case, they're gonna have to tow it back to the closest railroad yard—"

"Oh, for crying out loud! ... Isn't there another train?"

"No."

I'm stunned by the conductor's laconic, yet oddly calm, reply. For a split second, I don't say anything and look him straight in the eye. "That's it?"

At first, he doesn't stir. Then he glances at the other passengers, shrugs his shoulders, and snickers.

"Is everybody fine with this?" They're all sitting there, their faces blank as blinds. "Nobody has anything to say? You have absolutely nothing to say, is that it?" Not a word or a single syllable or even a grunt comes out of their mouths. "Why are you looking at me like that? Say something, goddammit!"

"Calm down, sir," the conductor says.

My legs give out. I keel over on the bench like a marionette whose wires have been snatched.

The conductor rushes to help me. "Are you all right?"

I try to speak, but he interrupts me: "You have got to take it easy."

"Sorry," I gasp.

"Don't worry," he says with an emphatic sweep of his hand.

* * *

After the awkwardness of the moment, the passengers resume what they were doing, which isn't much really. Most are mumbling to each other; some are smoking; and a pair are stretched out on the dirty floor, using folded hand towels as pillows.

The conductor is the most active of the lot, so to speak. At least he's trying to get some updates on the switcher from another employee, who has one eye that doesn't really care about the other. I feel bad for the poor bastard. It isn't wholly about the eye, though; he's also very short and angular, with disgustingly unctuous hair, and a toothless mouth, which he displays with great pride.

It occurs to me that I've completely forgotten to let Peppe know about the delay. He's probably waiting for me. I struggle to get to my feet, my knees still a touch frail, and drag myself to the public phone on the opposite wall. I dial Peppe's number. No answer. I try it a few more times, but to no avail. From across the room, I notice the conductor is still talking to the employee. I hang up the receiver and join them.

"Excuse me."

"What are you doing up?" the conductor asks, in a boisterous and overly dramatic tone.

At once, the passengers come out of their quasi-comatose state, their necks stretched out, their ears perked up.

"Sorry to bother you, but I have a little problem maybe you can help me with."

With his right hand, the conductor gestures to me to wait, not as much as a puff of air leaves his mouth. Then he turns towards the passengers, who, at the mere sight of him, instantly recoil.

"You were saying?"

"There's someone waiting for me, and I'd like to let him know about the delay. I was thinking maybe I could leave a message for him at the Figallia train station, if that's all right."

The conductor and the employee look at each other for a moment and exchange nods.

"Sure, I think that under the circumstances that'd be all right."

"*Appressu a mìa,*" the employee says, with his mouth wide open and a breath that could kill a horse.

"Sorry?" I'm trying not to stare at his eyes. Clearly he doesn't speak standard Italian.

"He wants you to follow him," the conductor says with a childish smile. I quickly mouth a thank you and go after the employee, who has already left without me.

I catch up with him in front of a personnel-only door to the right side of the ticket booth.

"*S'accomodasse,*" he says, accompanied by a hefty gesture, which I interpret as 'go ahead.'

The narrow and claustrophobic booth reeks of cigarettes and some other stench I can't really identify. There's a spindly employee inside, sitting on a swivel metal chair in serious need of oiling and arched over a mammoth logbook.

"*Prego*," the toothless employee says, aiming his soiled fingers at a desk, on the opposite side of the booth, with an oddly shaped telephone/intercom set on it.

The seated fellow lifts his eyes from the book and with the loudest screeching noise wheels toward us. I wince.

"May I help you?" he says. His furrowed brow exudes confusion.

I'm about to say something, but the toothless employee beats me to it. He passes me and gets closer to the other. After a brief exchange in their vernacular, the lanky one stands up and, to me, says: "Of course, no problem at all ... Follow me, please." He takes me to the funny-looking phone. "Where are we sending this message to?"

"The train station at Figallia."

"Figallia? I see ... And what's the message?"

"Um ... Nothing, simply ... That I won't be able to get to Figallia today and ... That probably I'll be there sometime in the early afternoon tomorrow."

"That it?"

"Yes, I think that's it."

"And who're we sending this to?"

"Yes, of course ... Mr. Giuseppe Tommasini."

"And who should I say this is from?"

"De Angelis."

He scribbles my name and Peppe's down on a piece of paper and reaches for an address book, which he quickly peruses. As soon as he finds the number he's looking for, he lifts the receiver with his left hand, places the right one on the keyboard but stops short of dialling it. He peers sidelong at me and says: "Anything else?"

"No, thank you."

"Very well, then." He points at the toothless employee. "He'll show you out."

I thank him and leave.

Chapter Three

It's almost nine o'clock, and some stubborn sunlight is still lingering, making the day seem interminable. Desperately in need of a stretch, I get up and pace around the waiting room. Still unsatisfied, I step outside onto the square in front of the station. It's a parking lot doubled as a coach terminal. Apart from a local bus, which is almost deserted, nothing moves; even the air is stagnant. I watch the dusty, ramshackle bus convulse and rattle away down the road. And just as it disappears behind a barren hill, I set off to the platform. It's one of those island platforms, slightly elevated with twin benches of the same type as those inside, sheltered merely by a rusty roof with open sides. An infantry of ants encircles a cluster of flies avidly feasting on the remnants of a panino thrown on the concrete right next to one of the benches, an empty garbage bin a stone's throw away. Rather than pick up the panino, I decide to let the flies have it. I'm heading back to the waiting room when I spot the conductor coming out. He stops two or three metres from the door. He lingers there for a moment, looking left and right. And after a quick body stretch and a tug on his pants, he goes into the small bar by the urinals —a few hops on the east side of the main entrance and, like the facilities, strictly accessible from the parking lot. A sudden pang of hunger drives me to follow him.

It's an incredibly narrow space with the counter taking up most of it, leaving little room to stand. The conductor, protruding belly and all, is smack in the middle of it, right arm resting on the counter, sipping an espresso with the other. I nod. He nods back.

"Do you have anything to eat?" I ask the barista, a scrawny ageless figure with dark and disturbingly deep eye sockets.

"Over there," he says, pointing at the far end of the counter, which I now realize is L-shaped. I thank him and make my way to the display. It's a little awkward though, with the conductor's clammy, malodorous back and mine brushing against each other, as I try to squeeze between him and the wall.

All I find are two day-old cannoli-shaped brioche, with a dull crust of custard sticking out from their extremities, and a solitary croissant, dry and pale and most likely just as old, on a silver tray covered with a grease-stained sheet of white paper. And next to the pastry, arranged in similar fashion, are three unctuous *Arancini*, frying oil having seeped through the cracked breading. I'm getting heartburn looking at them. "Is this all?" I ask.

"This isn't a restaurant," the barista retorts.

"You don't wanna eat that," the conductor says.

"It's not like I have many options. I don't have any more food."

"You up for a walk?"

He says there's a restaurant in town, or Trattoria rather, which the barista told him about. I don't have to think twice about it.

* * *

Much sooner than I expect, we find ourselves in the countryside in complete darkness, surrounded by nothing but olive trees.

"Are you sure you know where we're going?" I ask him. "I can't see a damn thing here."

"Don't worry," he says with an irritating chuckle.

Although not entirely satisfied with his answer, I keep quiet and carry on walking through the olive grove. At last, to my great relief, I detect some lights coming from a village not far ahead.

* * *

It's a small town indeed: two main streets, one wider and longer than the other, intersected at right angles with a few dead-end side streets, lined with terra-cotta tiled stone houses, ranging from one-story to three-stories high. We're walking up what the locals probably consider the actual main street, which has a higher concentration of stores, and it's also a little wider and longer than the other one. The church bell strikes nine-thirty. There's no one around.

If it weren't for some eerie stares, which I catch a glimpse of behind shutters, this could be a ghost town.

"There it is," the conductor says.

"Where?"

"There. See the sign above that door?"

"Yes, and?"

"Well, that's it."

What he referred to as a sign is merely a dark brown wooden plank with something daubed on it, which I'm able to decipher solely once we get closer. It reads: Trattoria.

A living room turned into a restaurant. That's what it looks like. There are five tables in total—three on the left side of the entrance, and two on the right side—with pink tablecloths and modest cruets of olive oil and vinegar as centrepieces. On the right side of the wall facing the entrance, there's a rudimentary bar; and next to it, on the left, a door frame with a beaded curtain, which I assume leads to the kitchen and toilet. Except for a couple of football banners and a tiny crucifix, the whitewashed walls are barren. As we're standing by the door, an obese lady with abnormally varicose ankles approaches us.

"Evening," she says.

I manage for a moment to lift my eyes from her ankles, only to notice that her bosom is hanging so low it touches her navel.

"Evening," we reply in unison.

"Would you like to sit down?" Her small hooded eyes seek the conductor's.

"Yes, please," he says.

"Follow me."

She rotates her large frame almost in place and slowly

shuffles to a table. After gesturing for us to take a seat, she disappears behind the beaded curtain and reappears a few moments later with bread sticks, bread, and butter. "I'll be right back," she says and vanishes again.

I'm surprised to see we aren't alone in the restaurant. Two men, each hunched over a glass of red wine, sit diagonally across from us, whispering to each other; and another man stands at the bar, sipping a digestive liqueur, his curious stare betrayed by the bar mirror.

"She forgot to give us menus," I say.

"They don't have menus here. Only dishes of the day." And flashing a stupid grin, he adds: "Trust me, it's good."

I had already sensed he lied to me, but that confirms it. For someone who claimed to had just learned about this place, he seemed a little too comfortable finding it, not to mention strangely too familiar with its peculiarities. I don't know why he felt compelled to conjure up such a silly lie. What do I care if he's been here before? I really don't see the point in all that, considering we hardly know each other. Anyway, I decide not to mention it lest I spoil dinner.

"We have a very nice stew tonight," the obese lady says, having somehow sneaked up on us.

"Stew? It's at least forty degrees in here. Don't you have anything lighter than that?"

Her face contracts like a veal cutlet thrown on a hot grill.

She looks to the conductor. "What's his problem?" she squeezes through her teeth.

"We'll have the stew and some red wine. Thank you," the conductor says in the smoothest way possible. She looks asquint at me and walks away without a word.

* * *

"So, what brings you to Sicily?" he asks, as I return from the toilet.

"Business."

"Business? What kind of business if you don't mind my asking?" He shoves a spoonful of stew in his mouth.

I don't want to talk about my work, so I hesitate answering him.

"Maybe I'm being too nosy. You don't have to tell me if you don't want to. We can talk about something else, all right?"

"No, no, that's all right," I say to avoid making a big deal out of it. "The company I work for specializes in fertilizers. We deal quite a lot with the island, actually. I'd say that most of our best customers are from Sicily. Anyway, because of the volume of shipments to the island and the obvious costs, the company is considering opening a branch down here."

"And you're supposed to make this happen?"

"Right."

"You're a big shot!"

"Not really."

Glancing over to the bar, I notice a slightly dishevelled man I hadn't seen enter standing there, checking himself out in the bar mirror. He isn't the one who was there earlier. He's definitely taller; also, he has on a different suit.

"Excuse me," the conductor says, getting up.

I nod and watch him being swallowed by the beaded curtain. As I stoop over my glass of wine, which is making me drowsy, I hear the tinkling noise of the beads. It's the lady coming my way. She asks if I want a cup of coffee or a digestif. I decline both and tell her I want to wait for the conductor.

"You sure?" She takes the empty plates off the table.

"Yes, I'm sure."

"All right, suit yourself. He'll be a while though."

"What do you mean?"

She ignores my question and walks back to the kitchen.

* * *

The wait is killing me. It's been over half an hour, and still no sign of him. One of the two men still sitting at the table diagonally across from me gets up and makes towards the beaded curtain. Past it, he goes straight to the toilet, for I hear him opening the door, which produces a distinct squeak. That's it. I can't take it any longer. I stand up and go to see what's going on. I knock. A voice that is not the conductor's answers.

"Sorry," I say.

I look about for other exits. Aside from the one through the beaded curtain leading to the dining area and the one right before it accessing the kitchen, there aren't any others. With no further option, or at least no better one that I can come up with at the moment, I stride back to the kitchen and barge in. The obese lady is standing by the sink, trying to unclog it with a gigantic plunger. As I move a little closer, I spot from the corner of my eye a wizened little man holding a magazine—her husband I assume—sitting on a stool by a set of stairs, leading to the upper floors.

"Where is he?" I blurt out.

She brandishes the dripping plunger at me. "What're you doing back here?"

"Where is he?"

"What's he talking about?" the little man asks, standing up.

"The man I was having dinner with, where is he?" I reiterate, enunciating every word.

"It's none of your business," she says. "Go back inside."

I'm about to fire back at her when I hear heavy steps coming down the stairs. It's him.

"What's going on?" he asks, tucking his shirt into his pants.

"Out of here. Both of you," she bellows. In that very instant, I hear the creak of a door coming from upstairs. I glance up. A girl who cannot be more than twelve hides behind the rail, half naked, looking down at us.

* * *

We leave the restaurant, not a word spoken between us. I don't want to broach the subject, even though all I can think about is the child leaning on the banister, her exposed pubescent breasts showing through the pickets, her deep, dark round eyes staring at me. To avoid eye contact, I let him walk several feet ahead of me. He obviously knows what I'm doing, but, aside from a few glances back at me, he doesn't seem too worried.

Despite the dense silence, occasionally disrupted by the solitary hooting call of an owl, and the sinister atmosphere, it's a lot easier to walk through the olive grove this time. The vapours rising from the soil, now damp and warm, combined with the complicity of the fat moon's rays shining through the tangle of branches have formed a low uncanny-looking mist.

Back at the waiting room, I think it best to go to sleep immediately. Most of the passengers are out for the night already, except the two soldiers who are playing cards with great animosity by the teller's window, away from the benches. As I lower myself on the bench, I notice the old lady's absence, as well as that of her luggage and the little dog. Someone must've come to pick them up while the conductor and I were away. I glance over to him. He's lying on the floor as far from me as possible within the confines of the waiting room, his broad back to me.

Falling asleep turns out to be impossible. The uncomfortable benches, the unpleasant chartreuse light coming from the fluorescent fixtures above, the heat, and the countless mosquito bites don't help.

No matter how hard I try, I can't stop thinking about that child. The whole scene keeps replaying in my head as if in a ceaseless loop, but each time it starts over a detail is lost, another one is gained or merged. During the wee hours of the night, the recollection becomes so slippery and amorphous the sole thing remaining strikingly vivid is the child's stare. It's only by early morning that, physically and mentally exhausted, I'm able to fall asleep.

Chapter Four

"*To all passengers, the regional train to Ponte Rotto will leave from platform two in fifteen minutes … To all passengers, the regional train to Ponte Rotto will leave from platform two in fifteen minutes,*" a distorted voice coming from a loudspeaker announces. I slowly hoist myself up. As my eyes adjust to the already high and scorching sun, I realize that the passengers and the conductor are gone, their luggage too. Nothing but heaps of cigarette butts and garbage remain. I peek at my pocket watch: 10:15. I'm not surprised no one bothered to wake me up. I'm actually relieved I don't have to face the conductor anymore.

Aside from an emaciated station agent behind a glass screen with a tiny window, I'm the sole person in the waiting room. I step outside onto the train platform. It's also deserted. The loudspeaker crackles, and a high-pitched screeching noise follows:

"*To all passengers, the regional train to Ponte Rotto will leave from platform two in ten minutes … To all passengers, the regional train to Ponte Rotto will leave from platform two in ten minutes.*"

I look across, right, and left. There's no sign of any train anywhere. I stand there for a few moments longer.

Back inside, I approach the station agent to ask him about the bus schedule. At first, he doesn't even acknowledge me. He's reading some kind of document, held up high, hardly a centimetre away from his face.

"Excuse me?"

He lowers the document and half turns in my direction.

"Yes?" he says with a grunt. His thick-framed spectacles make his eyes appear enormous.

"Could you tell me when the next bus to Malabbina is?"

"Three-thirty," he says and immediately brings the document up close to his face and with his index finger scrolls down the paper to find the point where he left off. He mouths the words like a child learning how to read. Suddenly he stops, his eyes fixed on the paper. "Yes?"

"Sorry to bother you again, but is there anything earlier than that?"

"There's a *littorina* around three. But the bus is a lot faster."

"Is that all?"

"Where're you headed exactly?"

"Figallia."

"Figallia? ... I see ... No, what you wanna do is go to Palermo instead. There are a lot more connecting lines there. You can catch the express bus at noon."

"And that doesn't stop at Malabbina?"

"*Express bus.*"

"I see. I have one more question if you don't mind."

The loudspeaker crackles again:

"*To all passengers, the regional train to Ponte Rotto is approaching the station ... To all passengers, the regional train to Ponte Rotto is approaching the station.*"

"Go ahead," the agent says, seemingly unfazed by the unpleasant noise of the loudspeaker.

"Yes, well ... um ... How do I get a refund for my ticket?"

"What ticket?" he asks.

I show it to him and explain what happened.

"I don't know anything about that."

"Look—"

"*Ciccio!*" the agent screams while moving away from the glass screen. He opens a door and shouts through it: "*Veni 'cca.*" Few seconds later, the cross-eyed employee shows up. As soon as he recognizes me, he gives me a big toothless grin. I nod and smile. The two start yelling at each other in tight vernacular. For a moment, I think the argument is going to get physical. Shortly after, however, they calm down a bit, and I can decipher some of what they're saying. It seems that the station agent scolded him for not reporting anything on the train's mechanical problem. In any case, they appear to come to some sort of understanding, and the agent moves towards me. He reaches below the counter and grabs a paper.

"Here. Fill out this form and mail it to this address."

I thank him and move away from the glass screen.

* * *

I follow the agent's advice and wait for the express bus to Palermo. It's five past twelve when I finally spot the bus pull in the parking lot and come to a rest by the platform. I collect my stuff and hurry to it. There aren't many commuters on the coach, mostly men and all sitting in the back. I have no idea which side of the bus is going to be shaded on the road, so I pick a random seat closer to the front. Within five minutes, we're on our way to Palermo. Fortunately, I've chosen the right side. As I watch the endless expanses of country scenery wheezing by, my eyelids get heavier and heavier, and, still fatigued by the lack of sleep of the previous night, I doze off in the span of ten to fifteen minutes.

In Palermo, one hour and fifteen minutes later, I immediately search for a ticket agent. There are none as far as I can tell. Not even a designated kiosk, bus shelters, or benches for that matter. All the buses are double or triple-parked on the street. I ask the first driver I come across if he knows which one is the connecting line to Figallia. He redirects me to another driver. I soon find out, not without disappointment, that the connecting bus to the village is still a little more than an hour away. Tired of carrying my luggage around, I inquire whether there's place where I can leave my belongings. He mentions the railway terminal. I thank him and walk to it.

The train station is housed in a stunning neoclassic building situated in the bustling Giulio Cesare square, around the corner. Inside it, I hunt for a locker. It doesn't take me long to track one down. I jam my bag into it and go find a place to get something to eat. But with purely fast-food eateries scattered throughout the terminal, I expand my search outside the station, hoping for better options.

Thankfully, I don't have to go too far. There's a little restaurant a few short crossings away. It's nothing fancy really, but it smells good, and the patrons, mostly locals, seem to enjoy their meals.

As I'm standing by the door, a waitress, in her early teens, signals me to wait. She's taking an order at a table. As soon as she finishes, she approaches me. "*Bongiorno.*"

"*Buongiorno.*"

Big black curls frame her milky and lightly freckled face, accentuating emerald-green eyes.

"Please, follow me."

She takes me to a table by the window, hands me a menu, and darts away before I can even say 'thank you.' However, no sooner do I sit down and open the menu than she comes back.

"What can I get you?"

I don't have the heart to tell her I haven't had a chance to take a good look at the menu yet. "What do you suggest? … I'm not from around here."

"I hadn't noticed!"

I have to say I'm caught a little off guard by her caustic remark.

"Would you like to try something traditional?" she asks.

I nod.

She convinces me to have pasta with sardines, or *paista chi saiddi* as she calls it, a typical dish of the area. I don't like it. It's too fishy for my taste. Anyway, I don't want to disappoint her, so I don't say anything.

I observe her for a while. Everything about her body language seems inappropriately sensual: the confidant, almost cocky way she holds herself; the way she taps the pencil on her bottom lip and, at times, sucks on it; how she purses her lips in a self-satisfied, nearly devious smirk; and how she playfully pulls and coils a lock of hair around her finger.

"Is everything all right, sir?" a nasal feminine voice asks.

I slowly gaze left and up in the direction of the voice, which belongs to a sweaty lady wearing a soiled white apron. I run my eyes up and down her figure without saying anything. She resembles the young waitress, only older by about twenty years. She's also a good twenty to thirty kilograms heavier. A noticeable moustache blemishes her otherwise beautiful face.

"Is everything all right, sir?" she repeats.

"Yes, thank you."

"You've hardly touched your food."

"My eyes were bigger than my stomach, I suppose."

"I'll say."

"Excuse me?"

"I'd like you to leave, sir."

"What? Why?"

"I think we both know why."

I look away, searching for the waitress. She's standing next to a burly man, his face heavily sunburnt, his eyes virtually hidden behind sagging palpebral folds. The teenager's and the husky man's hefty stares are both levelled at me. Uncertain what to do, I take out my wallet.

"That's all right."

"I'm sure this is all a misunderstanding."

"I'm sure it is."

I try to lock eyes with the waitress one more time, but the lady swiftly moves over to block my view.

I get up and leave the restaurant at once.

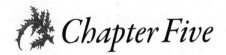 *Chapter Five*

I t's a little over two-thirty, and we're still in Palermo. The bus is filled with passengers. It's hard to believe so many people are going to Figallia.

"*Attention please,*" the driver announces into a crackling microphone. "*Please be informed that there has been a route change. This bus will not, I repeat, will not make a stop at the train terminal of Figallia. Because of a criminal investigation, the whole area has been closed off. All the busses have therefore been diverted to the local bus terminus up at the New Quarter in Figallia ... Also, for those continuing their journey beyond Figallia, a temporary kiosk has been set up. There, you'll be able to collect all the information you need to find your connecting lines. S.I.T. Autolinee wishes you a safe journey and thanks you for your patience.*"

Some of the passengers' reactions to the news is probably not what the driver expected. They stand up, come out of their seats shouting in outrage, and crowd the front of the bus, demanding more explanation. "*Please, step back everybody,*" the driver shouts into the microphone. "*Get back to your seats. Now!*" The passengers sheepishly comply. "*Thank you ... As I said, in Figallia you'll find all the information you need to continue your journey. You will all be able to reach your destinations.*"

And without another word, the driver puts down the microphone. In a minute's time, we take off.

***

"Yes, the red one."

"This one?" the bus driver asks, cigarette bobbing up and down in his mouth.

"No, I'm sorry. I meant the other one further back."

He gives me a displeased glance, as if it's my fault the suitcase has ended up at the far end of the luggage compartment. I didn't put it there. He did. Resting his left arm on the bus, the driver takes a deep drag on his cigarette and throws the rest away. Then he rolls up his sleeves, pulls up his pants, and crawls inside the compartment.

"Here," he says, pushing the suitcase.

I take it and step back. He re-emerges with his hands and especially his pants covered in grease stains, mostly around the knee area. I immediately check my luggage for marks. There are none. He takes a handkerchief out of his pocket and rubs his hands and trousers with it, all the while cursing and swearing. He doesn't seem to have much luck with the stains on his pants though. After shutting the luggage compartment, he goes back into the bus, still uttering all kinds of profanities without once repeating himself.

The bus engine starts with a high-pitched abrasive noise followed by whooping hiccups and clatter. The driver steps outside, looking in all directions to check for any late passengers, I suppose. There's nobody in sight. He goes back into the bus and drives away amid rattles and rumbles.

The bus terminal is located outside the core, slightly uphill and overlooking the town. I don't know why they call it the New Quarter. Not counting the freshly paved yet unfinished square—bulb-less lampposts and topless concrete bench ends along the edging, treeless round plant-beds in each corner, and a waterless fountain with an empty pedestal in the centre, what stands before me is anything but new. Across the piazza, two identical nondescript low rises, most likely subsidized housing, show premature signs of decay. Several discernible cracks, some re-surfacing from previous manifestly inadequate patching and others, perhaps, a touch too close to structural points, spread wildly on both fronts, and rust covers the majority of the balcony rails.

For edifices in such state, the two buildings seem dangerously overcrowded. Like threads in a loom, clotheslines packed with hanging laundry run from one building to the other on each floor. The balconies double as storage units with boxes, pieces of furniture, and all kinds of trinkets amassed on them. The parking area all around and in between the buildings teems with automobiles, three-wheeler pick-ups, crew-trucks, and motorcycles.

I lift my luggage and walk downhill on a dusty pebbled road towards the centre of town. On either side stand row houses, all the same size and all unfinished. A couple of them are barely skeletons. The rotted-out walls and the collage of penises and crude pornographic sketches graffitied on them indicate that nobody has been to these work sites in a long time. As I come upon a yellowed and slightly torn notice posted on one of the perimeter fences, I learn the sites were temporarily shut down due to a criminal investigation a little over a year earlier.

It's almost four, and the sun's relentless ferocity and the humidity brought by an unyielding sirocco make me woozy. Thankfully, the town is not too far ahead, and on the way to it before the bend I come across a water fountain. I wet my handkerchief, put it over my head, guzzle down some water, and continue down to the village, which from above resembles a terra cotta-tiled sea.

As I pass the long and steep bend in the road, the whole village comes into view. I hadn't realized that on the south side its border drops abruptly onto a ravine. The jumbled houses at the edge cling onto the walls of the gorge.

Unlike the one of the previous night, this medieval village inclines and has a maze-like layout with porticoed passageways and ramps of steps. It takes me a while before I'm able to reach my accommodation, which is located on a residential street on the north side of the village, comprised mostly of party-walled stone houses.

"*Via* Cavour 35," I whisper to myself, as if to make sure I've got the right address. I'm disappointed with the state of the lodging. It's neither a hotel nor a motel, not even a *pensione* for that matter, but a private home: a narrow, two-story house in complete deterioration, flanked by two massive constructions, of recent build, which almost threaten to squeeze it out.

I climb a few uneven steps and hammer the brass

knocker. No answer. I knock again. Nothing. I discover a tiny buzzer on the doorframe and press it. Again, no answer. Stepping away from the house, I notice that the jalousies on the second floor are a tad ajar. I could swear they were shut when I first arrived. I march back to the door and pound on it.

"If you don't stop, I'll call the police," shouts a feminine trumpet-like voice coming from the second floor.

I look up. Wrapped in a shawl, a tiny face with severe features is sticking out the window.

"Go away!" she says and makes to close the blinds.

"Wait! Wait! Wait a second. I'm here for the room."

"I rented it."

"You rented it?"

"Stop bothering me, or I'll call the police."

She pulls the shutters.

I stand there, speechless, staring at the window and hoping for God knows what. I turn, triggering a glissando of closing blinds. No one in sight. A doleful silence follows.

* * *

I wander around in search of a public phone and a place to rest. With the exception of some youngsters horsing around and some daring elders venturing out in this heat, the streets are by and large as deserted as they were on my way to the lodging. After a few dead ends and a couple of vandalized phone booths, both covered with graffiti and with broken doors — one missing the headset, the other one missing the entire apparatus, I arrive at the main square of which I had earlier caught a glimpse from a side street.

The piazza is exceptionally large for a village of this size with a stunning steepled Basilica towering over it; and, as far as I can tell, it's also where almost everything else is —the post office, the bank, shops, bars, and restaurants. The rest of the plaza, except for an amateurish bust of Garibaldi at the very centre, is spare and mostly flat with a slight hump in the middle and edged only with a few pine-green benches.

One by one, I check the bars for payphones, but no luck so far. The two restaurants are not open yet, and there's one last sports bar left to search. It's a questionable one, with umber wainscoting above which a plethora of football banners, scattered from corner to corner, cover the hardly visible faded-salmon walls.

"Do you have a telephone here?" I ask the open-mouthed barista, who's standing behind the counter leafing through betting slips. At first, he gawps, as though stunned; then, he aims his Habsburg jaw at the wall right beside me, opposite the counter. I turn around. All I see is an upright, single-glass-door display refrigerator with a single chocolate-ice-cream cake placed onto the middle rack. I glance back at the barista.

"Behind the fridge," he says, anticipating my question.

I nod and walk to it.

I call Peppe several times. Still no answer. I sit on a white patio chair that's scarred with cigarette burns. Tiring summer tunes play on a scratchy transistor radio by the counter.

After draining two tall glasses of water, I order a tea with granita to satisfy the barista's overly exacting, and certainly not subtle, gaze, but also in the hope of keeping him away from me for a while. He strikes me as the logorrheic type.

Why would the landlady rent out a room that's been already fully paid for? Surely Peppe must've told her about the delay? It's even too late to call the office in Milan at this point, and certainly it seems a little premature to bother Montanari with it. Running out of options, I decide to leave the bar and look for Peppe's house, since I have his address with me, and perhaps wait there until he gets home.

* * *

"Excuse me, do you know where *Via* Garibaldi is?" I ask a youth zigzagging on a bicycle.

"Two streets down turn right, first cross street turn left," he shouts. Then, with almost no effort, as if suspended with an invisible string, he lifts the front wheel and steadily pedals down the square completely oblivious of any possible incoming traffic from the intersecting streets.

It turns out the boy lied to me. Where he sent me is not only the wrong the street but also not even close to *Via* Garibaldi. It takes me a couple of wrong turns and the minute directions offered by an eager passer-by to find Peppe's place.

It's a three-story construction of modest build with a plain light grey façade, somewhere in the middle of the west side where the village slopes up a bit. There are some partially used building materials out front. All the blinds, from the windows to the walkout doors on the balconies, are shut. There's clearly nobody home, but I give it a shot anyway. I go heavy on the buzzer, which is so loud it shudders the morbid stillness weighing over the street.

"There's nobody there," a female voice says from next door.

"Excuse me?"

I look for the voice and notice the left side of a two-panel venetian blind slightly angled open.

"They're not home. Stop ringing the bell!"

"Do you know when they're coming back?"

"They went to the country house. I don't think they're coming back tonight."

"You sure?" She closes the blinds. "*Signora*? Are you still there?"

No answer.

* * *

After waiting in vain for about an hour in front of Peppe's house, I walk back to the bar I was in earlier and ask the barista, for there's no one else, if there are any hotels in town or if he knows anybody who could take me in for the night. His face lights up. He's probably been dying to ask me a thousand questions from the moment I stepped into his establishment. He immediately dismisses the possibility of a hotel or anything of that sort.

"Figallia is too small of a town for that. But not to worry," he says with the smugness of a child. And then he goes on and on about all the possible people who could take me in. After the fifth name, the fifth life story, and umpteenth digression, I interrupt him: "Could you get me in touch with one of those people? You seem to know them all very well. I suppose any of them will do. I trust your judgment."

Though my awkward attempt at flattery doesn't strike the right chord, the barista, visibly irritated by my interruption, reaches for a phone behind him, next to the cash register. "What are you doing down here without a place to stay, anyway?" he asks.

"It's kind of a long story. Let's say that I had a room, but there must've been some sort of misunderstanding between the landlady and the person who arranged it. Anyway, I don't have it anymore."

"Who arranged it? Someone local?"

"Yes, as a matter of fact."

"Who, if you don't mind my asking?"

"Not at all. He's name is Peppe ... Peppe Tommasini."

The barista's face turns ashen. He stops dialling and slowly puts down the receiver.

"I'm afraid I can't help you, sir," he says in a strangely low register, his eyes cast downward.

"What? Why?"

"I don't know anybody."

He picks up a rag and starts cleaning the already pristine counter.

"What do you mean, you don't know anybody? Not even two minutes ago you described the whole town to me."

"I don't know. I like to talk. I talk to talk, that's all. Now if you don't mind?" And goes on with his pretend cleaning.

* * *

With no place to go, I plan to retrace my steps to the bus station, up at the New Quarter, hoping to catch a coach back to Palermo. There I know I won't have any problem finding a hotel, and I can call the office in Milan first thing in the morning to straighten things out. It's past seven when I head back, and the town has suddenly sprung to life. A feebler sun and a more forgiving breeze have brought people out into the streets, or on their balconies, and street vendors have mushroomed on almost every corner. Their litanies weave with the buzz of three-wheeler pick-ups and Vespas shooting in and out of side streets. In the piazza, the wheedling, sardonic voice of the fritter-seller and the smell of fritters have lured a stream of townspeople, avidly lining up to get a hot bite of *panelle*, as he calls them.

It doesn't take too long to find my way back to the pebbled road, for the New Quarter is quite visible from down below. Again I'm surrounded by nothing but fractured columns of fibrous cement, rusty iron rods, and crumbling stacks of tufa overgrown with weeds. The slanted rays of the sun shining through the fissures and openings of the unfinished buildings cast a grid of light and shadows along the path. Barks, muffled by the unrelenting shrill of the cicadas and the raucous cry of crows, echo in the distance.

As I stop at the water fountain to freshen up, I notice a pack of stray dogs coming around the bend at the bottom of the road. There are six or seven of them. I look to see how far the bus station is. It seems kilometres away. I turn back to the dogs, hoping they've changed their course. On the contrary, they've picked up speed. Growling and barking is all I can hear now. Even the cicadas have gone mute. I grab my luggage, more out of a motor impulse than anything else, and make a beeline for the station. I look back to check on the dogs. They're gaining ground. As a diversion, I let go of my luggage. It works. They stop and circle the suitcase like blow-flies, snuffling and stabbing their fangs into it. But once they realize there's no food in it, the pack resumes the hunt, leaving a couple behind to finish the job on the baggage.

One of the dogs, the leader I assume, moves a lot faster than the others. As it gets closer, I recognize the triangular-shaped pricked ears, the pointed muzzle, and the chestnut coat. It's a *Cirneco*, a rabbit hound. I won't make it to the bus station. But not too far ahead stands a perimeter fence with a slight incline. I sprint towards it. By the time I reach it, however, the hound has caught up with me. I hear heavy panting and snarling right behind me. I freeze in mid-motion with hands and right foot on the fence. Afraid to so much as breathe, I remain as still as possible. Meanwhile, the other dogs have caught up as well. Now it's me they're circling. When their baying reaches deafening decibels, I know they're ready to charge. With a sudden move then, I try to climb over the fence. Sharp fangs rip through my pants and dig deep into my flesh. I jerk my leg to shake the dog off. But I lose my grip and fall to the ground. Flat on my back, I cross my arms over my face and kick my legs in the air to keep the hounds at bay. Two shots ring out. The dogs wail and whimper. Two more shots ring out. The moaning grows distant. A hand touches my arm. I push it away with a spasm.

"You all right?" a voice asks. I'm still kicking. "Calm down. They're gone, you're safe now. Stop!"

Chapter Six

"**T**his is going to hurt," the doctor says, a ghoulish glint in his eyes. I don't flinch. I study him, as I lie down on the medical exam bed, trying to make sense of his features: his thick uneven eyebrows, low and prominent; his right, owl-like eye, set lower than the other; his thin lips, trapped in a perpetual smirk; and his aquiline nose, twisted heavily to the right. It's like glancing at an optical illusion. As the needle pierces my flesh, I clench my jaw. The doctor looks up. I avert my eyes.

The space, a study turned into a consulting/emergency room, showcases an array of folders and medical books scattered around in stacks, a cheap reproduction of Rembrandt's anatomy lesson, and what I can only hope are antique surgical instruments. Someone knocks. The brass handle turns and the door whines open. A bleary-eyed frail figure appears behind it carrying a large tray. Her hair is fastidiously partitioned in the middle and neatly coiled up in a bun; her complexion, pasty. She wears an embroidered ankle-length skirt and a matching shawl draped around a beige turtleneck.

"My sister," the doctor says, answering my curious stare.

She has brought us two tall glasses of almond milk and a panoply of homemade cookies.

"You have to try the almond paste," the doctor says, proffering the plate of pastry with his left hand, grabbing one for himself with his right.

"I can't."

"Nonsense."

"All right. Just a little one."

"So? How is it? ... The cookie!"

"Oh, it's ... It's good."

"Good?"

"It's very good. Excellent."

The doctor gives a sidelong once-over at his sister—who's within earshot, padding around the room with a slight stoop—and says: "Well, at least that ugly spinster is good for something."

Finished with the stitching, the doctor slouches back in his seat and grabs another cookie. The sister promptly shows up with sterile bandages. The doorbell rings. They look at each other for a moment. And after handing over the bandages, she flees the room. Not even a minute later, the door flings wide open, and the sister comes rushing back in.

"Alfonso, the *Carabinieri* is here," she says with a grotesque vibrato in her voice.

"The *Carabinieri*? Here? What for?"

She makes to answer but hesitates.

"What?" the doctor says. "What is it? Talk ... Goddammit, speak, you old stinking bat!"

She throws me a quick glance, moves closer to the doctor, and whispers something in his ear. He looks at me from under his shrivelled brow. Then he takes his gloves off and walks out.

The sister stays with me. She stands there, stiff, her eyes even duller, a light film of sweat covering her face, as if waxen.

"This way, *Brigadiere*," the doctor's brassy voice says in the hallway. "Please." He ushers the *Brigadiere*, a stocky man with ballooned cheeks and a nonexistent forehead, into the room.

A full minute of slippery stares, throat clearing, and restless limbs follows.

"Concetta, coffee," the doctor says. "Cookies, *Brigadiere*?"

"With pleasure."

"Almond?"

"That'd be wonderful."

The doctor claps his hands twice, and the sister excuses herself.

The *Brigadiere* takes a chair and sits across from me. "Mr. De Angelis, is it?" He criss-crosses a handkerchief over his face.

"Yes. How do you know my name?"

"How's your leg?"

"It's fine. But how do you know my name?"

"How's he doing?" he asks the doctor.

"Good, considering. He's lucky it was the fleshy part of the thigh! ... Anyway, the wound is all stitched up, and I also gave him a rabies shot. That reminds me, don't forget your follow-up shots, Mr. De Angelis."

I nod.

"Can he walk?"

"Yes. Nothing strenuous, of course."

"All right then, Mr. De Angelis. Whenever you're ready."

"Ready for what?"

"The *Maresciallo* wants to see you, straightaway."

"The *Maresciallo*? Why?"

"He'll clarify that to you in person," he says while sloping his upper body to one side. "Is that your luggage back there?" he asks, pointing at it with a tilt of his chin.

"Yes."

"Those dogs did quite a number on it! Is there another pair of trousers you can wear? The ones you're wearing are ripped pretty badly."

"I don't know." I slide myself to the floor, limp to the baggage and rummage through it. "The clothes at the bottom seem fine."

"Very well. Whenever you're ready, Mr. De Angelis."

* * *

At the barrack, the *Brigadiere* has me waiting in some kind of foyer.

"Take a seat. I'll be right back," he says and disappears behind an armoured door with a tiny thick-glassed window.

Half-hour later, I'm still waiting. I thought he said the *Maresciallo* wanted to see me straightaway. It's almost nine and the last few shafts of sunlight coming from a large north-side window barely light the Spartan waiting area. A predominance of dark grey tones, from the ceiling to the floor, give the room a claustrophobic feel. I sit on one of those uncomfortable metal folding chairs. There're six of them: three on my side, and three across alongside the armoured door. And apart from a short stack of torn *Carabinieri*'s magazines resting on a small side table to my right, the room is completely unadorned.

The *Brigadiere*'s flickering eyes crop up behind the small window. The door rattles open. He offers a hollow apology for the long wait and takes me straight to the *Maresciallo*'s office.

Eugenio Pennone, reads the nameplate.

The *Maresciallo* sits behind a colossal—I'm pretty certain non-standard—leather-top mahogany desk, which clashes with most of the décor: two large leaden-tinged archival shelving units, arrayed on either side of the desk; and, alongside the opposite wall, as part of a light-walnut set, an armoire, topped with towers of bulging folders, an escritoire with a straw chair, and, under the window, perpendicular to the entrance, a coffee table paired with a couple of aged-leather armchairs—also, I'm assuming, non-standard.

On the wall, beyond the *Maresciallo*, along with the *Tricolore*, crucifix, a photo of the president and some other smaller banners and placards, there are several frames of different sizes and materials all sporting, I presume, key figures in the *Carabinieri*'s highest ranks.

I sit opposite him. Broad shoulders, giant hands, beetling brow, and bushy moustache make him look massive and threatening. There's a young *Appuntato* by his side, sitting on a squeaky stool to the left. He looks infinitesimal next to his boss. The *Maresciallo* seems absorbed in a heated phone conversation, but I can tell he's sizing me up from the corner of his eye.

He hangs up the phone. "Thank you for coming, Mr. De Angelis," he says.

I nod.

"First off, I'd like to clarify that this is not, by any stretch, an interrogation, shall we say? No charges have been filed against you. Of course, we don't know what the future holds."

He pauses, looks me square in the face, and roars with laughter.

"What charges? What are you talking about?"

"Anyway," he says, after his whole body stops quaking. "There's no need to worry."

"I'm not worried."

The *Brigadiere*, who's been hovering at the edge of my peripheral vision, sidles up to the desk, standing next to the *Maresciallo* and across from the *Appuntato*.

"Oh, good. Good. Very good," the *Maresciallo* says, exchanging sour glances with his underlings. "I'd like to ask you a couple of questions if you don't mind."

I don't say anything.

"How's your leg, by the way? You know, it's ... it's appalling what happened to you. In this day and age! I bet these kinds of things don't happen in the north, huh? What am I saying? I'm sure there are crazy dogs over there too, aren't there? I don't know, it seems ... and I'm not basing this on any scientific study or anything, although this so-called science, my dear De Angelis ... let's just draw a pitiful veil over it. Anyway, it seems to me that Sicilian dogs are angrier, shall we say? Although—"

"I thought you wanted to ask me a couple of questions."

The *Brigadiere*'s and the *Appuntato*'s faces freeze, twisted like Venetian masks, in a disquieting and almost comical grimace of dismay.

"Yes, of course," the *Maresciallo* says, shifting in his chair and running his thick fingers through his grey speckled hair. "Does the name Filippo Mancuso mean anything to you?"

"No."

"What were you doing at the train station of Colasberta?"

"The train broke down. I was actually forced to spend the night there."

"Can anyone confirm this?"

"What? That the train broke down? Why don't you call the *Ferrovie dello Stato*?" The *Maresciallo*'s face turns flinty. "You can ask the station agent. Small man. Cross-eyed."

"One more question, and then you're free to go. What is the purpose of your visit?"

"Business."

"What kind of business?"

"The company I work for is trying to purchase a lot."

"Who's your contact down here?"

"Giuseppe Tommasini. But I haven't been able to get in touch with him yet."

"I see. Well, I'm afraid that's not gonna happen."

"And why's that?"

"Did you send this?" the *Maresciallo* asks, producing a small piece of stationery with something scribbled on it.

"What is it?"

The *Maresciallo* hands it to me. It's the message I sent

with the help of the toothless employee to Peppe, just yesterday.

"So?"

"Yes, it's mine. I couldn't reach Peppe over the phone, so I left a message for him. But why do you have it?"

"We found it on Tommasini's body."

"Body?"

"Giuseppe Tommasini and Filippo Mancuso were shot dead yesterday in plain daylight inside the train station here, outside of Figallia."

"I ... "

"That's all for now, Mr. De Angelis. The *Brigadiere* will take you to your lodging."

"I'm afraid I don't have a place to stay. Apparently, the landlady decided to rent out my room, which was fully paid for."

"Did she?"

"Yes."

"Don't worry, the *Brigadiere* here will handle it."

"I don't know. She seemed quite firm on it. She wouldn't even open the door."

"Firm, you say?" The *Maresciallo* and the *Brigadiere* squint at each other. "Well, let's see if we can change her mind," the *Maresciallo* says, barely able to finish his sentence before erupting into another and even bigger guffaw. The *Brigadiere* follows suit. "We'll talk some more, Mr. De Angelis," he manages to spit out between fits of phlegmy cough. "We'll talk some more."

* * *

The *Brigadiere* double-parks in front of the lodging. "Wait here, Mr. De Angelis," he says, eyeballing me through the rear-view mirror. "I'll be right back." This he says to the young *Appuntato* sitting in the front passenger seat. He wrestles himself out of the armoured Jeep, goes around the back, and walks to the house.

Through the car windows, I can clearly see him approaching the door, climbing the steps, and pressing the buzzer. Without waiting nearly enough, he presses it again. The door cracks open. He's talking to someone, most likely the landlady, but I can't see her. It's also impossible to hear what they're saying from inside the Jeep. All I can tell for sure, judging by the *Brigadiere*'s vexed body language, is that the landlady is not caving in easily. He stops talking and nods as if in assent to something. The door closes, almost all the way. He leans with his right hand on the doorframe, fidgeting with his fingers.

The radio in the vehicle crackles, and the faint and somewhat distorted voice of a dispatcher drones something unintelligible. A strident beep ends the brief radio communication. The door reopens; this time I can see the landlady. They have another exchange, a short one; the tone of it is definitely more conciliatory. He nods, again in assent to something, moves away from the door, and walks back to the Jeep. He opens the door to my left and says: "All right, Mr. De Angelis, everything is good now. Get your stuff."

 *Chapter Seven*

"**M**r. De Angelis," a muffled and slightly echoed voice calls from the hallway. A violent knock follows.

Half asleep, I sit up and examine the crack across the stuccoed ceiling. Maybe it's my imagination, but I have the impression it's gotten bigger overnight. A dusty shaft of sunlight, coming from the large window clothed in silk damask, spills over the opulent chest of drawers.

"Mr. De Angelis," the voice repeats. It's the landlady. I recognize her harsh, almost vulgar, tone, except this time it has a fatter quality, more like that of a flugelhorn than a trumpet.

"Come in."

She yanks the door open and stands there, black-clad, looking askance at me.

"Yes?"

"There's a call for you. Phone's downstairs by the entrance. Make it quick. Coffee?"

"Yes, please."

She half nods.

"Make it quick," she reiterates before slamming the door.

* * *

"Hello?"

"Hello, De Angelis?"

"Yes. Who is this?"

"Montanari—"

"Ah, Mr. Montanari, of course. I—"

"How was the trip?"

"Not too good, I'm afraid."

I sit down on a tiny sculpted stool next to a heavily carved hall tree stand with a bevelled oval mirror.

"Told you, you should've taken a plane. You know I love you, De Angelis, but sometimes you can be stubborn as a mule. Didn't I tell you not to take the train? Didn't I? Huh?"

"Yes, you told me."

"You damn right I did. Anyway, how's Peppe? ... Hello? De Angelis, you there?"

"Yes."

The shape of a wavering tree projected on the white wall across from me attracts my eye.

"Did I catch you at a bad time?"

"No, no."

"Then what is it? Speak, for Chrissakes!"

"I hate to be the bearer of bad tidings."

"Please, don't tell me the deal's off already. You just got there. Didn't Peppe talk to these people? Did you do exactly as we talked about? I can't believe this, goddammit! How pigheaded are these people?"

"Peppe's dead."

"Come again?"

"Peppe—"

"What do you mean? He's dead? How?"

"He's been shot."

"Shot? By whom?"

"I don't know." The shadow of the dancing tree disappears. The landlady's elongated contours show in its stead. "Look, I can't really talk now, but I'll call you as soon as I know a little more."

"All right. Call me right away if you hear anything."

I hang up the phone and turn my neck. She's standing hardly a metre away from me, stony-faced, her hands spooned over her stomach.

"Coffee's ready," she says. "You done?"

"Yes, thank you."

I get up and go straight to the kitchen. I don't want to spend more time than I have to in this place. Once in the kitchen, I'm actually surprised to see that along with coffee she has prepared a generous breakfast. There are biscuits, freshly toasted bread, three kinds of preserve, and croissants. I want to thank her again, but she has already left the house.

* * *

After breakfast, I cruise around the village, trying to figure out my next move. It was Peppe who was supposed to arrange the first meeting with the Colantonio brothers, the owners of the property, to facilitate the negotiations. I eventually stop in the main square. The discomfort in my leg has turned into searing bouts of pain. I walk to the nearest bench and collapse on it. The pain subsides almost immediately.

I scrutinize the Basilica for a time. From where I'm sitting, it seems to me the church has two distinct sections: the west door, characteristically Arab-Norman; and the east end, late Roman, early Byzantine. But the structural modifications have been so skilfully done it can easily fool the untrained eye. Its beauty is accented by the stark contrast with an abhorrent, angular construction, still underway, erected a few doors down at the corner with one of the capillary streets branching out from the square.

While pondering the church's splendid design and on who would build such a monstrosity so close to it, I notice a pair of kids playing football around the bust of Garibaldi, or rather, pretending to play football, slowly getting closer to me. Their conspicuous glances betray them. I feign obliviousness and watch them carry on with their little scheme. It's play-acting at its best. One of the two kids, the dominant one, no doubt, is so immersed in his performance he's faking anger at the other one for being such a lousy kicker. At one point, he even grabs his friend by the shirt collar and, with perhaps the least subtle movement I've ever seen, kicks the ball in my direction. He runs over to me. I take the ball and spin it in my hands a few times. The little boy stands, inert, two to three leaps away from me, his eyes squinted in distrust.

"Look what I found," I say. "I think I'll keep it."

The boy keeps his eyes planted on me. Meanwhile his little friend has joined us, half-hiding behind him. "This is a great ball, isn't it?"

"It's mine," the boy cries, in a mixture of anger and fright.

"Oh, I see. Do you want it back?" The boy makes as if to move. The other one pulls on his shirt to stop him. Wrenching himself free, the boy starts towards me but yields almost instantly, as if overcome with scepticism. "What? You don't want it?"

"Fuck yourself!" he shouts.

"Hey! Go wash your mouth, *curnutieddu*," a croaky voice behind me bellows.

The boy freezes and shrinks, his fearful gaze cast beyond my shoulders. For a moment, he struggles with indecision. Then, with a daring and swift move like that of a feline, he jumps at me, grabs the ball, and runs away with his little friend tailing right along.

"De Angelis, right?"

I turn to the voice. It belongs to a sunburnt man in his forties, with a ruby-veined bulbous nose. A farmer judging from the shreds he's draped in and the smell of cow shit. I hesitate answering him. He knows my name, but I can't place him.

"It's nice to see you up and about already. How's your leg?" he asks.

"Are you ... ?"

"I suppose I am."

"I never got to thank you for rescuing me from those dogs, Mr. ... ?"

"Calò."

"Sorry, I didn't recognize you—"

"Don't worry. You were in shock."

"Still. Thank you."

"Ah, don't mention it ... Kids!"

"What?"

"Kids. You've got to love them."

"I was only fooling around with them."

"You waiting for someone?"

"No, I was just admiring the church."

"Beautiful, isn't it?"

"Yes, very ... It's amazing to see how it evolved over time. The transition from the due east—Late Roman, early Byzantine I'd say—to the Siculo-Norman façade is quite remarkable."

"An architect or something?"

"Who? Me? No ... I mean, technically speaking."

"I don't follow."

"I never took the state exam."

"I see ... Well, Mr. De Angelis, I'm not even gonna pretend I'm as knowledgeable as you about churches, or architecture for that matter, but ... I do know one thing: Whoever did the work on this basilica knew exactly what they were doing. Unlike those swine responsible for that eyesore over there."

"I'm sure it'll be better once it's finished."

He lets out a boisterous laugh. "I'm afraid that's finished."

"But it's still under construction!"

"My dear De Angelis, no one is ever going to set a foot in there."

"Why not?"

"Seventy percent sand." I don't say anything. "That's right. Seventy percent sand! ... Come on, let me buy you a coffee."

* * *

Of all the bars—and there are a remarkable number of them for such a small town—clustered around the main square, Calò has chosen the same one I went to the previous day. The barista, loquacious as ever, is torturing four poor fellows. But as soon as he lays eyes on me, he stops talking. The four men, suddenly mere silhouettes, crab out of the bar, soft-footed. We order two espressos and sit outside.

"What do you think of this?" Calò asks, unfolding a piece of paper he takes out of his jacket pocket.

It's a page torn from a newspaper. "What am I looking at?"

"Bottom page, right-hand corner."

Calò directs my attention to a small article about the shooting at the train station. Above it, there are two pictures: Mancuso's on the left, and Tommasini's on the right. Peppe's face is nothing like I expected it to be. I can see, however, why Montanari couldn't get a better description of him. Peppe has one of those faces that are hard to define. He's neither handsome nor ugly, with nothing prominent about his features, as if lacking any character.

"Why are you showing this to me?" I ask him.

"What did the *Carabinieri* say to you?"

"How do you ... ? Never mind."

"So?"

"Nothing, really. They didn't even mention it was a Mafia hit, let alone that Peppe was involved in *Cosa Nostra*."

"Because he wasn't."

"He wasn't? That's not what the article is hinting at."

"I suppose, it depends on how you view it. In a few days, I assure you, it will emerge that the real target was Mancuso, not Tommasini. And nobody will contest that, especially the

Carabinieri. You see, dear De Angelis, there will be no doubt that Peppe was no more than collateral damage, so to speak. Wrong place. Wrong time. When it is in fact the other way around."

"I'm not sure I'm following."

"You see ... Mancuso must've thought he was the bait. But what he didn't know—I'll bet my shirt on it—is that he was also the sacrificial lamb."

Calò pats his jacket, reaches inside it, and takes out a pack of cigarettes. He offers me one. I decline, saying: "You know what's funny? While talking to the *Maresciallo*, I had the impression he thought I had something to do with this."

"No, he doesn't." He smiles and shakes his head from side to side. "He sure wants you to think so, though."

"Why?"

"Officially speaking, nobody wants you and your Milanese company coming down here and exploiting our land, our people, and, God forbid, make a profit off of us. You see." He leans in slightly. "This is what's been crafted and fed to this mindless herd. But what they are not telling them is that they are scared shitless of what your bulldozers might find, if you get my meaning. Now whether you believe me or not doesn't really matter." He takes the article, folds it neatly, and puts it back in his jacket pocket. "But allow me to offer you a piece of advice. First of all, don't mention a single word to anyone about this. It won't do you any good anyway. And second of all,"—he gets up —"just play along and at the first opportunity get the hell out of here."

Chapter Eight

Since Calò left, I haven't been able to bring myself to move, his words still ringing in my head. I've been staring at the same cup of coffee for God knows how long. I'm not certain what to make of Calò, but the whole affair strikes me as too elaborate to be perceived as mere scare tactics; and Peppe's death does appear a little too coincidental. Either way, I should definitely get in touch with the owners of the property, if anything, to test the waters.

Gazing at the clock on the steeple, I notice it's almost noon and finally summon the strength to get up. As I do so, three-wheeler pick-ups, crew-cab trucks, and tractors start crowding the square. Landowners and field workers step out of them. They move in clusters, shouting either pleasantries or derisive remarks at each other and slowly disappear into the bars. The church bell strikes twelve. A siren, like that for an air raid, goes off. I look around more confused than alarmed. A trio of latecomers hurries across the piazza. Someone should probably tell these people

WWII is over. As the excruciating sound of the siren gradually dies out, the workers re-emerge from the bars in twos and threes, and almost in unison, as though led by a shared innate impulse, they light up the last cigarettes before lunch.

It dawns on me that lunch hour is probably a good time to call the Colantonio brothers; the contact number I have is that of a private residence. I swing back into the bar. The barista is chatting away on the phone behind the counter. I signal to him that I want to use the payphone. He doesn't even acknowledge me and looks the other way. I use it nonetheless; it's for the public after all. I call the Colantonios, but the phone rings non-stop. I hang up and give it a go one more time. No change. I head back outside.

The sun, sizzling high above the campanile, radiates into every nook and cranny of the piazza. The short canopy I'm standing under provides no shade at all. Not hungry exactly but needing to lie down a while, I go back to the lodging.

As I try to open the front door, I realize the landlady must've given me the wrong set of keys, for they don't fit into the padlock. I don't want to pound on the door, given her reaction last time I did that, so I press the buzzer—just a couple of times, and with enough time in between to avoid upsetting her. No answer. I look up. All the jalousies are shut.

"*Signor lei*?" a man shouts behind one of the shutters across the street. "Don't go away. I'll be right there."

I try to figure out exactly which window the voice came from, but the sun's too bright. A whole minute elapses before I hear the tinkling of keys and the clunk of a dead-bolt sliding open. I put a hand above my brow to fend off the light. A man in shirtsleeves and suspenders strides towards me. The sun bounces off his brilliantine-smothered hair. He's sporting a bushy moustache—hung over his mouth, the extremities curled upward—something between a walrus and a handlebar. As he gets closer, the smell of menthol tightens my throat.

He introduces himself as a relative of the landlady and is kind enough to let me inside the house. He happens to have a spare key with him. He insists on preparing coffee for the both of us, even though I don't want one. The coffee is obviously only an excuse to talk to me. He rattles on about his cousin, the landlady, whom he resembles quite a bit, but unlike her he has a somewhat charming lightheartedness about him. After the second coffee that I once again decline and several cookies I don't touch, he asks me if I want to have lunch with him. I try to get out of it.

"I don't feel comfortable using the kitchen," I say.

"Ah, that's all right," he replies. "We can go to my place."

"I was also going to check the stitches in my leg. It's been hurting me—"

"Oh yeah. A stray dog bit you, right? I heard about that."

"Did you?"

"This is a small place Mr. ... "

"De Angelis."

"You can't even take a dump without it making it to the front page of Figallia's bulletin ... There you go! That's the spirit! Smiling is very therapeutic, you know."

"Yes, I think I heard about that."

"Do you want me to have a look at the stitches? With this kind of weather, you wanna make sure it's nice and clean."

"That won't be necessary. I'll be right back."

***

"*Gesù*, Giuseppe, *e* Maria!" Turiddu—that's his name—
struggles with the lock. "It needs to be at the right angle,"
he says. Beads of sweat form below his hairline and slowly
branch down his temples. The key slides into the lock. He
gives it a big turn and pushes the door open. A light rattle
echoes in the pitch-dark entrance hall. A complacent smile
overspreads his face. As we step inside, the stench of boiled
chicken hits me in the face.

"Wait here for a moment," he says and trots upstairs.

It takes a while for my eyes to adjust to the dim lighting; and my lungs, to the smell. Regaining full vision, I give
my surroundings a good once-over. The entrance hall, the
hallway, and the visible part of what appears to be the
salon are crammed with perfectly preserved eighteenth and
early nineteenth century furnishings—at least, by the looks
of it.

Footsteps come rolling down the stairs. It's Turiddu.

"Totò," cries a drawn-out raspy voice upstairs.

Turiddu stops midway without turning, his head dropped
back. "Don't forget the sponge," the voice says. Turiddu
takes a deep breath and slowly brings his head back up. His
eyes cross mine. He offers me an unfinished smile and
continues down the steps.

"My mother," he says, patting my right shoulder.

At a loss for words, I feign sympathy with a head-bob.
He seems pleased with that. We go through the hallway,
Turiddu a step ahead of me. On either side hang several
paintings, all portraits with heavily carved frames. Giuffrè
is the recurrent family name on the paintings' nameplates.

In some of them the title of Count precedes the name. A sudden urge to ask about the portraits and the furniture assails me. I refrain.

Passed the hallway, the salon, and two closed doors, I spot the kitchen to the left.

"Go ahead," Turiddu says, gesturing towards it.

It's a medium-sized room with no window and mismatched appliances. Humidity stains, mould, bubbling and cracked paint cover the walls. A lone light bulb hangs from the ceiling. We sit at a round table—massively thick, judging by its legs—right in the middle of the room, under the turbid light. A bunny-patterned vinyl tablecloth with embroidered hems stretches across the table. Over it lie neatly stacked lottery tickets, charts, notebooks, a ruler, a pencil, an eraser, and a calculator.

"I suppose I should put these away," he says. I put on a one-sided smile and keep quiet. Palms flat on the table, Turiddu lifts himself up, collects the lottery tickets and the stationery and stacks them, pausing in between items as if making sure they are in the right order. In place, he takes a quick scan of the room, I assume in search of a spot to put the papers. Eventually, his flickering eyes land on a dresser off to the left of the door we came in. He pelts to it and, gently, lays the pile down.

"Do you play lotto?" he asks while approaching the refrigerator.

"No, not really. Sometimes, I suppose."

He reaches for a deep dish, lifts the tin foil covering it, and sticks his hand right into it.

"It's almost ready," he says. "Do you like *Pollo Tonnato*?"

"I don't know. I mean, I've never tried it."

"You've never tried it?"

"I don't really like chicken."

Turiddu's face sinks in disappointment.

"Oh, I see. Well, I'm sure I can throw something together."

"Look. You don't really have to trouble yourself. I'm not even that hungry. Really."

"Nonsense," he says, quickly taking stuff out of the fridge. And before I can conjure up another excuse, an array of cold cuts, cheeses, olives, pickled vegetables, cured scomber, sardines, and two kinds of bread spread before my eyes.

* * *

"More wine?" Turiddu asks.

"What?"

"Wine. Do you want some more?"

"No, thank you."

"You sure?"

"Yes."

"I'll drink yours too, then ... You okay? You seem distracted. Is your leg still bothering you?"

"Yes," I say, lying to veer the conversation away from me. Perhaps I replied a little too quickly. I can see Turiddu's eyes narrowing a bit. "On second thought, I think I'll have some more wine."

This seems to satisfy him. He shuffles to the refrigerator, takes out another bottle of red wine, and sets it on the table.

"Where were we?" he says, fumbling with the bottle opener.

"I don't know. The mansion, I think."

"Right."

With his left hand clutching the bottleneck, Turiddu wraps the other around the partially extracted cork, pops it open and pours us a couple of brimming glasses. He drinks his in one gulp and like deadweight collapses in his chair.

"Where were we, again?"

"The mansion."

"Right. So yes, in the end we couldn't manage it any-more, financially speaking. And eventually we ended up in this dump, and my cousin across the street. You see, she was in a better shape than we were, money-wise that is. Her husband, *bonanima*, left her enough — should we call it re-sources? — to live off of, at least for a good while."

"How did he die?" I ask. I don't know exactly why. Turiddu hesitates answering me. "I'm sorry. I didn't mean to pry."

"That's all right. It's no secret anyway. Technically speaking, he's not dead."

"I beg your pardon?"

"He's missing."

"Why is she wearing widow's weeds, then?"

"My dear De Angelis, missing doesn't mean that he's coming back. He got mixed up with some bad people. Anyway, one evening he rushed out of the house, saying he had a meeting to attend, and he never came back."

"Totò," his mother calls out from upstairs. Turiddu doesn't move. He pours himself another glass and drains it.

"Totò," she cries again.

"Is she all right?" I ask.

"Ignore her. She's fine."

"If you don't mind my asking, how do you ... ? Never mind."

"What? Go ahead, don't worry."

"How do you get by? I'm assuming not by playing lotto."

"I'll have you know I have a system ... Anyway, to answer your question: Subsidies."

I give him a questioning look.

"I'm my mother's caretaker."

"I see." Turiddu reaches for the bottle again. "What happens when she dies?"

He looks at me for a moment, a sinister grin plastered across his face. "I won't tell anyone."

The doorbell rings. Turiddu excuses himself and rushes to the door. I stay in the kitchen. As Turiddu's bouncy steps fade away, the humming of the appliances and the slow but steady drip coming from the scale-incrusted faucet fill the room. Turiddu's voice and that of a woman's bleed through the hallway. I pay closer attention and recognize her voice. It's the landlady's. She's at the door quarrelling with her cousin for God knows what. Maybe she saw we used the espresso maker. I get up and move to the hallway door to listen better, but it's no use. They're arguing in tight vernacular. Just as I'm about to go back to the table, I hear my name. I try to listen again, but their voices have gone down to almost a whisper now. I step into the hallway to get a little closer, but, as I do so, I hear footsteps moving in my direction. Swiftly I run back to the kitchen and take my place at the table.

"De Angelis," Turiddu calls, standing by the door.

"Yes."

"My cousin's here. She says she needs to talk to you. A certain Montanari called. I don't know."

"Thanks for lunch," I say in passing.

"'Thanks for lunch'? You hardly touched any of it."

I don't say anything.

"We should do it again," he shouts.

"Sure," I reply.

The landlady is sitting in a cushioned chair by the door in the entrance hall. Our eyes meet, and immediately she gets up and steps outside onto the curb. I follow her.

After shutting the door behind me, I ask: "What did Montanari say?"

"He didn't say anything."

"What do you mean?"

"Nobody called."

"I'm not sure I'm following."

"Listen," she says, rummaging through her purse. "Here's the right set of keys. Sorry about that." A hint of a smile gathers at the corner of her mouth. "I know my cousin can be a little much." I make as if to speak. "Don't worry," she says before I can open my mouth. "You don't have to say anything."

A full smile takes hold of her face.

"I have to go now," she says.

Maybe I'm wrong, but I perceive a touch of regret in her voice. I watch her traverse the street—twice gazing at me shyly with her head cocked downward—and swerve into a side street a few corners down. I linger there for a moment longer. Except for a fruit peddler eating a sandwich under the merciful shade provided by an improvised canopy—the curtained right side of a truck rolled out and held up with two broom sticks—there is no one around. A mantle of silence, disrupted solely by the occasional clanking of pots, has descended over the street, which is simmering under the perpendicular sun.

I go to the lodging.

Clambering up the stairs, I have to hold on to the handrail at one point. I shouldn't have had that second round of wine. As soon as I set foot in my room, I switch on the little fan on the dresser and throw myself on the bed, trying to get some rest, but to no avail. The throbbing pain in my leg has spread to other parts of my body. Seeking some kind of relief, I reach over and wrap my hands tight around the wound. Rivulets of sweat race down my back. I gaze at the squeaky fan. It's blasting at full speed, but it's no match for this weather.

Chapter Nine

Despite the pain in my leg, I must've dozed off, for I'm jolted awake by the loud thud of the front door slamming shut. The whole house quakes. It must be the landlady. I take a hand towel from the chair next to the bedside table, wipe myself dry, put on one of the two surviving shirts the dogs didn't turn into shreds, and make my way down the steps and, in turn, to the kitchen, where I hear some noise. As I cross through the kitchen door, I inadvertently startle her.

"Sorry, I didn't mean to scare you."

"That's all right. I didn't hear you come in."

She moves to the oven, opens it, and places a deep tray covered in tin foil onto the middle rack.

"Is there something I can do for you?" she asks while shutting the oven door. And before I can even part my lips, she adds: "I'm sorry. I don't know where my mind is. I'm making myself a snack. Would you like some?"

"No, thank you."

"It's no problem."

"I'm all right. Really."

She leaves her eyes on me for a trice longer. Then she moves away and goes on to set the table. Still waking up from the short but deep sleep, I'm having trouble gathering my thoughts, so I stand there.

"What is it?" she asks with a tinge of anxiety. She stops what she's doing—folding a paper napkin, that is—and places her fisted hands on her hips. "Did that blabbermouth of a cousin say something he shouldn't have?"

"No," I say. Her body seems to relax a little. "I wanted to ask you if you know where the Colantonio brothers' house is? I have the address, but I don't know where that is."

"The Colantonio brothers? Why, yes, of course. I know where they live." She gives me meticulous directions.

Their house, or castle as the landlady calls it, is on the east side of the plaza. I thank her and go back upstairs, bolt the door, strip naked, drag a chair in front of the fan, and stick my face right in front of it. I down one of the elephant pills the doctor gave me for the pain and stay there for a while, waiting for the sun to go down a bit.

* * *

It's a quarter to six when I chance it outside the house. And though not exactly breezy, the temperature is already much more tolerable. Aside from a few kids racing on bicycles and the occasional encounter with a lifeless octogenarian standing at a street corner, the town is still by and large empty. Only the grating of steel shutters, coming from storefronts in the piazza, a hundred or so metres ahead, foreshadows any sign of life.

As I get closer, I can already catch a glimpse of villagers strolling about, some sitting on the benches, and others standing in groups. All the bars and shops seem fully ready for business, except for the two restaurants not yet open for dinner and the stationery/magazines shop, whose owner or worker is still organizing the newspapers on the display-stand outside the storefront.

I cross the piazza.

The Colantonio brothers' residence, located on a quiet, residential cul-de-sac, is indeed stately. Even if not the sole big house on that particular street, theirs stands out. It's a beautiful modern mansion, with tastefully blended accents of classicism, stretching four stories high.

One glance is enough to realize the residence is vacant. The windows on all four floors are shut. No laundry hangs from any of the balconies. No cars or any other vehicles are parked out front. And piled up correspondence, at least two days old, sticks out from the mailbox by the gated entrance.

I give it a try anyway and push the buzzer on the right side of the gate several times. As predicted, no signs of life inside it whatsoever. I walk away. As I'm about to head back to the piazza, I hear: "Psst."

There's no one in sight.

"Psst." This time, on the right side of the street, I spot a slit in a Venetian blind. I'm pretty sure that's where the sound is coming from. I move closer.

"Don't look directly at the window," the elderly voice says from beyond the shutter.

"Excuse me?"

"Face the wall and put your foot on it. Pretend like you're tying your shoe and take your time with it. But whatever you do, do not look at the window and keep your voice down. Understood?"

"Yes."

"Good."

"Can I ask why?"

"No! … Now, what the hell are you doing looking for the Colantonio brothers?"

"What do you mean?"

"What do I mean? I think you're smarter than that."

"I really don't know what you mean."

"They're gone."

"Gone? Where?"

"Doesn't matter, but they ain't coming back."

"I'm not sure what you're driving at here, but—"

"And if I were you, I'd do the same." The slit on the venetian blind shuts closed.

"Hello? You still there? … Mr.?"

* * *

Somewhat taken aback by yet another warning, I sit on a bench in the piazza to clear my head. There're too many wandering eyes for my taste. After a short while, I think it best to leave the square and drift around the village. I mostly dawdle on side streets hoping to avoid people as much as possible. It turns out to be futile. The streets, which were basically empty a few minutes ago, are now inundated with villagers, street-vendors, cars, three-wheelers, motorcycles, and whatever else is swarming about. Besides, the long walk is making me even more restless, and it's taking quite a toll on my leg.

I cut through an empty lot and walk along the first street I recognize that leads to the lodging.

Back at the house, I start upstairs to my room when I hear the landlady holler my name from the kitchen. I turn on my heels and move toward it, but she forestalls me by coming out to the hallway.

"Did you find the place?" she asks.

"Yes, thank you."

"Oh good, good. Listen, I didn't know what time or if you were coming back, so ... I already ate, but would you like me to fix you a plate? I can scrape up something."

"That's not necessary, I don't want to put you out."

"I insist."

"I was going to grab a quick shower."

"Half-hour, okay?"

"That'd be fine. Thank you."

She darts back to the kitchen.

Up in my room, I get undressed, cover my bandages with cellophane, and hop in the shower. The water, coming from a cistern up on the terraced-roof, has no pressure whatsoever and, because of the sun beating down on it all the day long, is so warm it offers no relief from the heat.

* * *

"Oh, there you are. Did it feel good?" She's at the kitchen counter, plating some kind of braised meat.

"Yes, thank you," I say, not wanting to upset her or seem rude.

She lowers the overflowing plate onto the table. "Have a seat."

I don't know what kind of expression I have on my face, but she seems pleased with it. A warm smile sprawls on hers.

We both sit.

"I hope this is fine," she says.

"This is more than fine. Look ... I'd like to pay for these extra meals. I know they're not included in the rental fee."

"Nonsense!"

"No, really, allow me—"

"Stop it. I won't have it. Plus, I wanted to apologize for the way I behaved yesterday."

"No need for that."

"It's just that ... When I heard about Tommasini getting shot ... I don't know if my cousin told you anything about my husband."

"Some."

"Anyway, I ... "

"You don't have to justify yourself. It's water under the bridge." I stab the fork into the meat and bring it to my mouth. She doesn't take her eyes off me. She smiles again. I reciprocate.

"Did you find the Colantonio brothers?"

I shake my head from side to side. "Do you know how I can get to the Colantonios' property?"

"Which property?"

"It's got a vacant warehouse."

"Oh, I see. It's the one by the old mill."

"Is there a bus I can take or something?"

"A bus? No. There's no such thing. You can borrow my car if you like. When do you plan to go?"

"I'm thinking tomorrow morning."

"No problem ... How's the food?"

"It's good, thank you."

"Do you mind if turn on the TV? My program's coming on."

"Please, don't mind me."

She bounces to her feet and crosses to the credenza. She opens it, uncovering a TV set. She reaches for the remote and turns it on. Back on her chair, she zaps through the channels until she finds the one she's looking for.

"Shoot! It started already."

It's a trashy Latin American *telenovela*.

 *Chapter Ten*

"**A**ny luck?" the landlady asks, having crept up on me.

"No. Still nobody home."

"Well, you should get some breakfast before you go," she says, walking away towards the kitchen. I hang up the phone and follow her.

While we eat, she gives me painstaking instructions on how to reach the property and, more importantly, on how to work the funky stick on the Charleston. She also tells me where to find the toolbox and the spare tire in case I get a flat, and where to gas up if I want to save a few lire.

As soon as I finish the last piece of toast, she hands me the keys to the car, which she lets me know is parked inside a garage across the street; she slides that key across the table as well. I thank her for breakfast and make as if to leave.

"Say, before you're off, do you have anything you want me to wash? I'm doing laundry today."

"That'd be lovely. If it's not a problem?"

"Not at all. Leave it outside your door."

"Sure."

* * *

The second I turn the key in the ignition, I know this is going to be a rough ride. It takes a bit of practice to get used to the stick on the Charleston, and I can't even get the damn thing started. Numerous tries later, I'm finally able to ignite the engine.

Even with the scrupulous directions the landlady provided, I still manage to lose my way. It's only after the third wrong turn that I succeed exiting Figallia and set off to the Colantonios' property, which, according to the landlady, shouldn't be more than twenty to thirty minutes away.

I'm pleasantly surprised with the first stretch of the route. It's not particularly wide, but at least it's pretty smooth, unlike the side road leading to the land that I steer the car onto. This second stretch isn't paved at all or even level; it's more like a rock-strewn path. This strikes me as quite odd. I recall reading in Montanari's notes that there should be an access road large enough at least for a semi-trailer truck. Maybe the landlady sent me to the wrong place.

I have to endure ten whole minutes of the bumpiest and dustiest ride I've ever been on before I spot the large warehouse, the perimeter walls with the gated entrance of the estate, and the service area/parking lot in front of it. It turns out the larger and official access road to the property runs along the other side of the estate. She must've given me directions to a short cut.

I drive through the chalky parking lot all the way to

the main access road. A shallow, dried-up riverbed covered with bone-white smooth rocks borders it. I swing the car around and drive back to the entrance and park next to it, to the left. I get out and walk to the tall gate. It's locked. A thick rusty chain, with a huge padlock just as rusty, hangs loosely between the two halves of the gate, but apart enough that someone petite could actually slide through. I take a closer look at the chain. I'd say it hasn't been moved for a long time; it's practically moulded to the corroded metal rods of the gate.

I notice a three-wheeler pick-up parked inside the walls by the warehouse; there must be another way in. Despite the considerable distance, I can clearly see someone getting on it. And within a minute or two, the three-wheeler starts driving down an overgrown track, clouds of dust trailing behind. It draws to a stop a few metres from the gate. I can't really make out the person inside the cab. The windshield is too dirty; the sun, too bright already.

The door of the three-wheeler shrills open. A relic of a man holding a cane emerges, and with a snail-like movement approaches me. It must be more than forty degrees, but he's wearing a dark brown wool suit, with vest and necktie. He stops about a metre from the gate and me. And with a slight quiver he switches the cane from one hand to the other. He's tiny, minuscule in fact. His face is withered like a sun-dried tomato, his eyes but a glimmer behind folds of decaying skin. From his back pocket, he takes out a handkerchief and repeatedly coughs in it. His whole body shakes. He wheezes heavily and makes sucking and gargling noises. A greenish phlegm spits from his mouth and lands hardly a few centimetres from his feet. He wipes his mouth and puts the handkerchief back in his trousers. He moves closer to the entrance, so close in fact I can smell his rotten breath. Then he reaches inside his jacket and, sticking his hand through the iron rods of the gate, passes me a folded piece of paper. It reads:

> Dear Montanari,
>
> We have considered your generous offer. However, it is with the deepest regret that we must inform you we have decided against selling. Please, accept our apologies for any inconvenience we have caused you.
>
> Best Regards,
> Marcello Colantonio

I look up. The old man is still standing there. His right hand is fully extended, palm flat and facing upward. I return the piece of paper. He puts it back in his jacket and walks back to the three-wheeler. I watch him drive away.

* * *

After stopping at a roadside hash house to use the toilet and cool off a bit, I head back to Figallia. Still en route, I spot in the rear-view mirror a white Fiat Uno with a broken left blinker, which I saw parked in front of the greasy spoon but also, and I'm pretty sure about this, earlier on while struggling to get out of town. A sign in the road indicates the presence of a gas station not too far ahead. I decide to stop. As I pull into the station and come to a rest in front of one the pumps, I keep lookout for the white car;

it wheezes by. Maybe I'm wrong, but I could've sworn that car has been following me all morning.

I wait a moment longer, to make sure the white car is gone, then bend to turn the key in the ignition. Out of the corner of my eye, I catch a bouncy filling station attendant, fast approaching the Charleston.

He leans in, bringing his face uncomfortably close to mine, his soiled navy-blue overall brushing against the door. "*Bon pomeriggio.*"

"Good afternoon."

"How much?" He extends his left arm for the keys.

I'm about to decline when the Fiat Uno pulls in the gas station.

"Sir? How much?"

"What?"

"Gas! How much?"

"Oh ... Um ... Whatever fits, thank you." I hand over the keys without looking at him.

As if in slow motion, the white car comes to a complete stop at the opposite end of the service area. Nobody comes out of it. From this far, it's impossible to identify the driver of the vehicle or to tell whether there's more than one person inside.

I can't take it.

At once, I jump out of the Charleston and, though hazy on why or what I intend to do exactly, march toward the Fiat. I'm not halfway there when the car speeds out of the gas station. And unfortunately, I'm not able to take a good look at the driver.

* * *

Back in Figallia, I drive straight to the lodging. There's a small envelope with my name on it taped to the front door. I open it:

> *Mr. Montanari called right after you left. He*
> *wants you to call him back as soon as possible.*

I, too, scribble a note for the landlady and leave it on the kitchen table:

> *Thanks for taking the message for me. And let me*
> *thank you again for lending me your car. It was*
> *very gracious of you. I also wanted to give you a*
> *warning. It looks like I might leave much sooner*
> *than anticipated, perhaps as early as tomorrow.*
> *Anyway, I'll keep you posted.*

Up in my room, I freshen up a bit, change my bandages and lie down on the bed. Not until the hottest hours have passed do I step out of the house again. It's a little over five when I make my way to the barrack, a few blocks on the other side of the square on the way up to the New Quarter.

Even before I can ring the bell, the intercom crackles —nothing discernible coming out of it—and the front gate buzzes open. I climb up the stairs three at a time. The waiting room is empty. I focus on the thick-glassed window on the heavy-bolted door. There's no one behind it. Since there's no buzzer or anything of the kind, and I don't think knocking would be appreciated, I take a seat on one of the folding chairs. Soon after, a loud clunk reverberates in the room, and the door half opens onto the foyer. I look up. The *Brigadiere* is standing behind the little aperture.

"*Prego.*" He clears the way to let someone else through first.

"Thank you," the other voice replies.

It's the conductor's.

My stomach drops to the floor, my lungs choke, my muscles jolt. As a reflex, I promptly hold on to the chair I'm in and, within seconds, manage to recompose myself. I keep my eyes glued to the door, breathing slowly and deeply to alleviate an upwelling nausea. The conductor materializes from behind it belly first, his face pointed at the exit across.

"Do you need a ride to the station?" the *Brigadiere* asks, not a trace of sincerity in his voice.

"No. That won't be necessary."

"Well, then. Thanks for coming, Mr. Morale."

"It was no problem at all. I was glad to — " He stops mid-sentence, as he finally sees me.

A thick silence cloaks the room. A moment or two later, although it feels much longer, the door rattles wide open, revealing the *Brigadiere* slightly stooped with his head outstretched like a turtle's, aiming my way.

"Ah, Mr. De Angelis," the *Brigadiere* says. "What a coincidence." And with an imbecilic smile stuccoed on his face, he adds: "I don't have to introduce you two, do I?"

I don't know why, but I reward the *Brigadiere*'s juvenile wit with a smile. I look at the conductor and nod. He nods back, his spherical face glacial.

"Well ... Again, thanks for coming, Mr. Morale," the *Brigadiere* says, cueing him to leave.

Caught unawares, the conductor utters some unintelligible sounds and with an awkward bow backs up towards the stairs. And before disappearing from view, he throws me one last inquisitive glance.

"What can I do for you, Mr. De Angelis? ... Mr. De Angelis!"

"What?"

"What can I do for you?"

"I'd like to talk to the *Maresciallo*."

The *Brigadiere*'s face shrivels, as if smelling something bad.

"You can talk to me."

"I just wanted to know if you need me to stay around a little longer."

The *Brigadiere* stands still, his eyes barely a fissure, his puckered lips moving from side to side, letting out but a bird-like sound.

"Wait here," he finally forces out of his contorted mouth, unable to disguise a deep-seated irritation.

* * *

"Please, do sit down, Mr. De Angelis," the *Maresciallo* says.

I take a seat in front of him.

"How's your leg?"

"Um ... It's ... It's ... I'm sorry. Do you need me to stick around or I can leave?"

"What's the hurry? Is there something we should know?"

"Excuse me?"

The *Maresciallo* and the *Brigadiere*, who is standing next to him, eye each other.

"Relax, Mr. De Angelis," the *Maresciallo* says, with a perfidious look. "I thought you were here on business."

"What does that have to do with anything?" I ask and immediately regret as Calò's words cross my mind. A dead-pan look is imprinted on both their faces. "But, if you must know, the deal fell through."

"That's too bad," the *Maresciallo* says, leaning back in his chair.

I sit there in silence.

"Well, I do have some good news for you, though. The *Brigadiere* here tells me you saw Mr. Morale on your way in."

"Yes."

"He was zealous enough to show up here, even though he didn't have to, and God knows we didn't ask him to. Anyway, he confirmed your story."

"What story?"

"You're free to go, Mr. De Angelis."

"What about Peppe?" I ask.

"What about him?"

"Is there any development?"

"I'm afraid this is an ongoing investigation, Mr. De Angelis," the *Maresciallo* says, affecting a sudden ill-suited professionalism. Then, with his eyes steady on mine, he leans in and whispers: "But, between us, from what we have so far, it seems that poor Tommasini was ... in the wrong place at the wrong time, shall we say?"

I don't say anything.

The *Brigadiere* escorts me out of the *Maresciallo*'s office and to the waiting room.

"*Arrivederci, Signor* De Angelis," he says, turning his back to me.

"Excuse me. If you don't mind, I'd like to thank Mr. Morale for coming down here. Do you know if he's staying in town?"

"He mentioned he was gonna try to make the six o'clock bus to Palermo." And after peeking at his watch, he adds: "That's in fifteen minutes."

I hurry to the bus station up at the New Quarter. I make it just past the bend in the road, but short of the water fountain, before stopping to catch my breath. A bark, even though far off, gives me a chill. I look around for strays. Not a single dog in sight. I forge on.

By the time I arrive at the bus station, it's three minutes to six, according to my pocket watch. There's one bus idling in the departure lane. The door is wide open, so I step inside. The driver's not there. I give the interior a quick once-over. There are a handful of passengers, but I don't see the conductor among them. To be sure, I slowly walk down the aisle scanning every seat. He's definitely not in any of them.

"Is this the six o'clock bus to Palermo?" I ask one of the passengers, an emaciated man soiled from head to toe.

Tight-lipped, he throws me a sphinxlike look. I repeat the question, thinking that maybe my northern accent confused him.

"May I help you?" a voice calls out behind me.

A well-groomed man with a shiny complexion is standing a few feet from me. He's the driver.

"Is this the six o'clock bus to Palermo?" I ask.

"This is it," he answers.

I move past him and make towards the exit.

"Where do you need to go?" he shouts.

I don't reply.

Off the bus, I stand at a safe distance so as not to be bothered by the driver, now leaning on the bus next to the door, looking intently my way.

It's well past six, and the bus hasn't moved. Neither has the driver. From his breast pocket, he takes out a pack of smokes and taps it a few times until a cigarette pops out. He takes it, twirls it, and brings it to his mouth. He's about to light it when something draws his attention. His head tilts up, and his gaze reaches past me, slightly to the right. He puts the cigarette back in the packet and hops on the bus. I look behind me. It's the conductor, dragging a piece of luggage in one hand and a briefcase in the other, rushing to the bus with an arrhythmic movement resembling that of a boat battling a sea storm. But as he spots me, he freezes.

"Are you getting in or what?" the driver yells from inside the bus.

The conductor looks up at the driver and answers with a quick nod accompanied by a nervous smile. He eyes me one more time before shuffling off to the bus. Visibly irritated, the driver steps outside, grabs the conductor's baggage and places it into the luggage compartment. The conductor grasps the door handle and, not without effort, lifts himself up all the while looking at me.

I can see him through the windows moving down the aisle all the way to the back and taking a seat on the side facing me. The bus door shuts closed. Without taking his eyes off me, the conductor opens the narrow sliding window in front of him. The driver must've pushed the ignition button, for the bus starts jerking and making choking sounds as if having some kind of seizure. It suddenly backfires. Murky clouds of burnt diesel spew out of the exhaust pipe and, aided by a gentle wind, wrap around the bus, drift upward, and hide, however briefly, the conductor's face. The bus door reopens. Only the driver's arm protrudes, reaches for the side mirror, and makes some quick adjustments.

"What do you think you're doing?" the conductor shouts, as he re-emerges from the smoke.

I don't know what to answer.

The door shuts closed again, and the bus rattles.

"Don't be stupid," the conductor says, his words immediately followed by the spine-curling noise of the gear lever. "You hear me?"

The bus takes off.

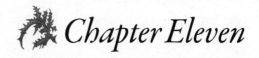 *Chapter Eleven*

"**M**ontanari's residence."

"Hello."

"This is Montanari's residence. Who's calling, please?"

"Is Mr. Montanari there?"

"He's unavailable at the moment. Can I take a message?"

"Um ... "

"Hello!"

"Yes ... Um ... Can you please tell him that De Angelis called?"

"Please, hold, Mr. De Angelis."

"Excuse me? ... Hello?"

Of all the pay phones in town, this seems to be the sole one in working condition and with no signs of vandalism. And for some cruel joke, it happens to be situated in the last bar I wanted to go to. I could've called from the lodging of course, but I'm in no mood for one of the landlady's prates. As I wait for some kind of response from the other end of the line, I give a sidelong gaze at the barista, whose unblinking eyes are planted on me. Suddenly aware of my own skin, I shake my limbs around as subtly as I can. A tingling sensation encircles my temples and creeps up towards the top of my scalp. I look away.

"Mr. De Angelis?"

"Yes, hello."

"I'm afraid Mr. Montanari can't come to the phone right now. When can he reach you at your lodging?"

."I'll call back later."

"Mr. De Ang—"

I hang up the receiver. Unwittingly, I pick it up again, only to slam it right back down. Aching to get out of the bar, I make for the door but stop midway. The barista is still watching me like a hawk from behind the counter. He's been polishing—I'm pretty sure—the same beer glass for the past ten minutes. I look over to the side. Amid spirals of smoke, a quintet of wheezing middle-aged men, who could stand to skip a meal or two, is sitting at a table, domed over their drinks and playing cards. Still feeling the barista's eyes on me, I glance back and take a few steps. At first, he doesn't flinch, but as I move closer he finally stops polishing that stupid glass. And as I get even closer, he lets the glass slip out of his hand onto the bar and takes a tentative step backwards. His body stiffens. A veil of apprehension draws over his face.

"What's so fascinating about me?" I ask him. The barista remains immobile, his lips slightly parted but soundless. "I know you can talk. So, tell me. What's so fascinating about me?"

A harsh symphony of squeaky chairs travels across the room. The barista looks past me, and within a second or two, the stench of beer breath and tobacco engulfs me. An annoying little song, supposedly a classic, plays on the transistor radio by the counter.

"Is there a problem?" a nasal and painfully drawn-out voice asks.

I don't say anything but slowly turn around.

An encircling wall of backlit figures is facing me. We stand there in silence, not a single move. Uncertain what to do, I think it best to get out of there, but I have to wrestle my way out, for there are no gaps between them.

* * *

For a long while, after leaving the bar, I limp around the village—the pain in my leg worsened by the run to the bus station—until I take a rest on a south-facing terrace dangerously protruding onto the valley as though suspended over it, with a shockingly low parapet to guard one from what would surely be a horrible death.

Sitting on a decrepit bench, I notice a spray of flowers leaning against the farthest east end of the wall and what seems to be a frame of some sort right below it. Bested by my curiosity, I walk to it. It is indeed a picture: the portrait of a man in his forties, with gaping eyes, an unnaturally craned neck, and the ashes of a frozen smile—a furtive sadness gathered at the corners of his mouth.

I cautiously lean on the parapet and stick my head out. The valley is nothing but tufaceous soil scarred by deep crevices stretching as far as the eyes can see. I'm staring at the myriad of fissures running through the bed of the valley when the cast of a large cloud moves in. I look up. An even larger and gloomier nebulous accumulation follows it, and within a minute or two the patch of sky right above me is fully curtained. As the thick, uniform layer of clouds advances further, spreading its edges in all directions, an ominous green-tinged billow mushrooms out of the flat mass. I can't help but stand there, looking at the darkening gassy formation pushing ever downward. Suddenly, swirling gusts of wind coming from every which way thrust me from side to side and almost push me into the precipice, as if the ground has been pulled away from my feet. I manage to hold on to the parapet and lower myself to the ground.

On all fours, I move away from the wall.

A muffled drone in the distance gets closer. It's a three-wheeler, grating and screeching to a halt not far from me. I turn around. An enormous figure with triple-chinned face is jammed inside the tiny cab.

"Are you all right?" he asks, blending the words together.

"I'm all right. Thank you."

"Need a doctor, or something?"

"No."

"You better find a roof. It's gonna come down any second."

I nod. He starts the engine and speeds away.

At the first raindrop, I decide to go back to the lodging. But by the time I reach the main square, cascades of rain and hail the size of tennis balls force me to seek refuge in a restaurant. I'm immediately greeted by the proprietress— late forties, slenderly contoured, with kind yet shallow eyes —who's standing by the door with a veiny kitchen helper right beside her, gawking at me. After an avalanche of platitudes about the weather, pneumonia, and the dangers of wet clothing, she escorts me to a table where some other poor wretches are sitting. We exchange nods.

"I'll be right back," she says and disappears behind a service door, merely to reappear a few moments later with an unjustified smile and a stack of clean, dry towels. She hands me one and points to the lavatory.

* * *

"Feeling better?" the proprietress asks, as soon as I return.

"Yes, thank you."

They all look at each other bobbing their heads approvingly. I smile. Sitting across from me, the proprietress scrutinizes my face to the point that I feel the need to shift position a few times. Then, as if remembering something, she bounces to her feet and goes to the kitchen. Relieved, I sink in my chair and close my eyes.

"Here. Eat this. It'll make you feel even better."

The proprietress has brought me a soup, fish judging by the smell. I hoist myself up and lean over it. I can see my face in it. I shake the bowl.

"Is there a payphone in here?" I ask.

"Yes. By the juke box. Don't you like the soup?"

I let out a few disjointed syllables, shake my head a bit, and excuse myself.

* * *

"Montanari's residence."

"Hello. This is De Angelis."

"Ah, Mr. De Angelis. It's good you called. Mr. Montanari has phoned your lodging a few times, but the landlady had no idea of your whereabouts. Anyway, please hold."

I peek at the table. The fellows hover over the soup with circumspect glances while the proprietress, no longer at the table, re-emerges from the kitchen, carrying an empty plate which, to the others' visible disappointment, she uses to cover the bowl.

"De Angelis."

"Hello?"

"Yes, hello. This is Montanari."

"Sorry to bother you at home. I know you don't—"

"It's quite all right. What's going on, De Angelis? I've been trying to reach you."

I look about me and lower my voice.

"I have some news about Peppe. It seems, although this is not official yet, that he was not killed intentionally—"

"What do you mean?"

"It appears that he found himself in the wrong place at the wrong time."

"You're kidding me. That's awful! ... How'd his wife take it?"

"I don't know. I haven't spoken with her."

"You haven't? For Chrissakes, don't you think that we should offer our condolences at least? When's the funeral?"

"I don't think it's set yet. You know, the autopsy and all."

"Of course, of course. Well, let's make sure we do something noticeable for the funeral. I'll wire you some money."

"Very well."

"What's going on the other front? Have you made contact yet? ... Hello? ... De Angelis, you there?"

"I'm sorry. Yes."

"So? Have you? ... Reached out to them, I mean."

"No."

"No?"

"Well, yes ... Sort of."

"'No,' 'yes,' 'sort of,' what the hell is this? What's with you? You either talked to them or you didn't!"

"Briefly."

"Care to elaborate?"

"We talked about Peppe. It didn't seem appropriate to discuss anything else at that moment ... Um ... However, in passing it was mentioned that perhaps we should resume talks after the funeral. I thought that was a good idea."

"Absolutely. Of course! ... Are you okay, though?"

"Me? Of course, why?"

"I don't know. You seem ... I don't know ... "

"I'm fine. I ... I didn't want to say anything, but the day I arrived I got bitten by a dog on my thigh—"

"A dog?"

"Yes. A stray dog."

"Why don't I know about this?"

"I didn't want to bother you with it."

"Jesus Christ! What in God's name is going on down there?"

"It's nothing serious. I'm just in a bit of pain. That's all. Look, I'll talk to them as soon as possible."

"Sure, sure, of course. Take your time. But first, make sure you take care of your leg."

"I will."

"Jesus! ... I don't know why, but somehow I can't help feeling responsible about this."

"Nonsense. It was purely bad luck."

"Even still ... Listen, I know this is a long shot, but did you get an idea if they're steering one way or the other?"

"Honestly, it was hard to tell."

"I figured. All right, keep me posted."

"Will do."

I hang up and linger there for a moment, my hand still clutching the receiver, the other one flat on the wall. Reflected on the metallic surface of the coin slot on the top right-hand corner of the payphone, I notice the distorted outline of a man approaching. The moist and deep, raisiny scent of shag tobacco precedes him. I pivot around and lean back a shade. An incredibly hirsute man wearing a yellowed undershirt has drawn up well into my personal space. His furrowed, bushy eyebrows and demeanour lend him the appearance of a pissed-off owl.

"You done with the phone?" he says, his voice even more irritating than his face.

Taken aback by the man's rudeness, I delay answering him.

"*O vucca 'perta*! You're done or what? I know you're not mute. I heard you talking over the phone. Do we got a problem here?"

I let go of the receiver and retreat hardly enough to let the man reach the telephone. He immediately hurls himself in front of it and grabs the handset. And as he starts dialling a number, he murmurs something in tight vernacular I can't make out. I move away.

I see through the window the hail has stopped. But the

rain shows no signs of slowing down, and with darkness closing in it seems even thicker now. I get back to my chair. The proprietress is at another table, her back to us. Quickly, I uncover the soup and give it to my companions in misfortune. At first, they hesitate. Then, in the span of a minute, they leave no trace of it.

Chapter Twelve

"**G**ood morning."

The landlady is sitting at the kitchen table embroidering what seems to be a centrepiece.

"Good morning," I reply.

"Coffee?"

"Yes, please."

She stabs the needle into the cloth, gently places the tambour on the table, and goes off to the stove. She grabs the *caffettiera*.

"I didn't hear you come in last night," she says, struggling to open the coffee maker.

"I was stuck in a restaurant almost all evening. The storm ... "

She reaches for a rag, dampens it, lays it over the bottom part of the coffee machine, and gives it a big twist, but to no avail.

"May I?"

She hands me the machine.

"I must've tightened it too much," she says and laughs nervously.

"There you are."

"Thank you." She goes back to the stove. "That was some crazy weather yesterday, huh? ... It did a lot of damage apparently. Vannino, the fruit peddler, you know, the one at the corner?"

"Yes."

"Well," she says, sitting down, "he told me that almost all the vines around the area were completely destroyed. Isn't that a shame? Even some of the hothouses were affected ... Vannino said that the hail was so big it made holes as big as a tennis ball. Imagine that."

I must be staring at her funny, for she gets all self-conscious suddenly.

"Anyway, the coffee will be ready in a minute. Do you want something to eat? I have beautiful ricotta *cornetti*."

"No, thank you."

"But they're really fresh, and the confectioner makes them with goat's milk ricotta only. They're really good."

"I'm all right really."

"Maybe some Indian figs? Vannino just gave me some. I bet you've never tried one."

I'm about to decline again, but I don't want to be rude, so I hesitate answering her. Thankfully, the percolating noise of the coffee maker turns into an ear-splitting whistle. She jumps to her feet, rushes to the stove, and pours me a cup. I drink it almost in one gulp. Mumbling a thank you, I move to the door. She looks at me as if wanting to ask me something.

I go first: "By the way. I won't be leaving, it looks like. Well, at least not for a few days."

"I was wondering about that. In the note, you mentioned you might be leaving soon, today even. What happened?"

"The *Carabinieri* still need me here. A formality they say. I don't know. It's probably for the best. It didn't seem appropriate to leave before the funeral anyway. I hope that's not a problem."

"Not at all. Besides, you still have a whole week left in your rental. You've been here for ... what? Two nights?"

"Right." I step into the hallway. "Do you have any idea when Tommasini's funeral will be held?"

"I was in the piazza this morning, but I didn't see the obituary posted yet. Then again, it was really early."

"Where is that?"

"What?"

"Where they post the obituaries."

"You know the church?"

"Sure."

"Well, it's right next to it. There's a little blind alley with a big board."

"Thanks."

"Will you be back for lunch?" she calls out.

"Um ... I don't know."

"You're more than welcome to."

* * *

As I step out of the house, Vannino, the fruit peddler, intones at the top of his lungs: "*Ficu D'Innia ... Ficu D'Innia frischi ... Ah, chi su beddi sti Ficu D'Innia ... Arrialati su ... Milli liri lu chilu ... Ficu D'Innia ... Ficu D'Innia frischi."*

He's leaning with his back on the truck, his elbows resting on it, his face lifted upward, basking in the still somnolent sun.

"Ficu D'Innia ... Ficu D'Innia frischi ... Beddi i Ficu D'Innia ... " he repeats.

"Do you have pears today?" a woman shouts from a balcony a couple of houses down.

"Pears? No. I got apples though. *Aruci comu lu meli."*

"How much?" she screams back.

"Milli e cincucentu liri lu chilu."

"What are you drunk already?"

"All right, all right. *Milli liri."*

"I'll take a case. I'll be right down."

I'm passing by the truck, and Vannino, who has moved to the other side of the flatbed, makes eye contact.

"How's one supposed to make a living like this?" he mutters.

"Excuse me?"

"Never mind," he says while preparing the case for the lady. I'm about to leave when he asks: "Did you make it all right yesterday?"

"What do you mean?"

"The storm. Did you get caught in it?"

"A little bit."

"That was some storm, let me tell you that."

"Right."

"Here. Have some of this."

Vannino hands me an Indian fig. I look at it.

"What's wrong?" he asks. "They're really fresh. I got it this morning."

"I'm not hungry, that's all."

Vannino glances past me, to the right, reaches inside the flatbed, picks up the case he has put aside for the lady, and comes around. I make as if to leave.

"Hold on," he says, placing the case onto a little tower of empty plastic crates by the flatbed. "I need to ask you something. Don't go."

When the lady arrives, she tries to drive the price of the apples even lower. They argue for a short while, but Vannino doesn't budge. Resigned and displeased, she finally shells out the money, and Vannino hands over the case.

"What is it you want to ask me?"

He waits for the lady to step away from the truck. "How's Teresa?"

"Who?"

"Giuffrè. Teresa Giuffrè. Aren't you staying at her place? I've seen you come out of her house for the past few days."

"And?"

"Are you a relative or something? You're obviously not from here."

"This is none of your business, now, is it?"

"You know, I'm not from here either. Every morning except Sundays, I drive almost two hours to get here. That's right. I park my truck in the same spot every day. Do me a favour. Look around you. There are way better corners in town than this one. Yet, I come here day after day."

"What are you driving at?"

"Teresa. She's nice, isn't she?"

"Sure."

"No. I mean she's *really* nice."

"Look. I'm here on business. That's all."

"You're right. It's none of my business," he says and goes to tend to a customer, who has just arrived.

Not sure what else to say to him, I leave it at that and walk away. Within a few minutes, I'm almost at the main square, which from where I'm standing strikes me as unusually crowded. It's a market. Rows of stands bristling with people are lined up in the centre of the piazza, surrounded by all kinds of vehicles—three wheelers, trucks, handcarts, and too many double-parked automobiles. The incessant hubbub of shouting, car horns and whistles is enough to drive anyone insane, not to mention the maddening litany of street vendors. But making things worse is the wet and pungent odour of fish thickening the air.

As my ears adjust to the noise level, I search for the blind alley the landlady mentioned. It's actually really easy to spot; it's contiguous to the church, on the left side. As I step into the alley, which is quite short, I find myself facing a big board covered with layer upon layer of obituary postings—an eerie, yet somewhat comical, collage of names and faces. And right there in the middle, still wet with thick tears of glue streaking across it, is Peppe's posting, the fresh ink slightly smeared. I move closer. It reads:

> *On July 6, 1987, at the age of 42, Giuseppe*
> *Tommasini passed away prematurely. The sad*
> *announcement is given by his devoted wife,*
> *Concetta; his only daughter, Marinella; his sisters,*
> *Raffaella and Elisabetta; his brother-in-law, Alfio;*

his nephews, nieces and relatives all. The funeral
mass will be held tomorrow, Friday, July 10th, at
3:00 pm in the church of Santa Maria degli Angeli
followed by the procession to the cemetery of
contrada Colafico.

Peppe's photo is the same one used in the newspaper article Calò showed me.

Chapter Thirteen

After stopping at the post office to collect the money wired to me by Montanari, I roam around searching for a flower shop. I find one in the outskirts of the town. It's not really a florist but a burial services shop, with a shimmering black hearse parked out front. A tawny, plump man in his forties with lustrous skin stands at the counter. There are other people in front of me, so I take a look around. I've never thought that the smell of flowers could be that nauseating. I'm not even sure what types of floral arrangements are appropriate for a funeral. It's not something I've dwelt on.

"*Bongiorno,*" a wheezy, almost lifeless, voice says.

A jaundiced skeleton of a man is standing behind me, heavily stooped over a knotty stick. Severe cataracts have fogged most of his eyes, sparing only the centre of the pupils and giving them an almost perfect elliptical shape, like a cat's.

"*Buongiorno,*" I reply.

"*A vostra disposizione*," he says, after a long, uncomfortable gasp. The words crawl out of his mouth drenched in saliva.

Between the thick accent and the slurred diction, I have no idea what the old man said to me. "I'm sorry, come again?" I manage to say.

The plump man who was behind the counter comes to my rescue. "Dad! ... What are you doing here?" he scolds. "Why are you bothering this gentleman?" Wobbling with disappointment, the old man lets out some jumbled noises. The son looks at me and says: "I'm sorry about that."

"Sorry about what? There's really no problem."

"Santuzza!" the son shouts, trying to hold his father still. "Santuzza!"

From an archway shielded with rainbow-coloured beads, behind the counter to the left, a feminine yet orotund voice comes thundering in. "What is it? Why are you yelling?"

A corpulent hand emerges from behind the beads, shifting them enough to reveal part of a silhouette. "What is it?" she repeats.

"Come get Dad."

"Dad? What is he doing there?"

The hand moves further, unveiling a massive figure with unkempt grey curly hair, unpleasant eyes, no neck, and a dress reminiscent of a red-checkered gingham tablecloth.

"I don't know ... He wandered in. What does that matter anyway? Come on! Come get him. I got people here."

Santuzza steps in sideways—not by choice—and trudges towards us, holding on to anything on her way.

"All right, Dad. Santuzza is gonna take you back."

I pick up dread in the poor old man's eyes. Quivering even more than before, he gives me a final look and slowly, very slowly walks away with Santuzza.

"How can I help you? ... Sir?"

"Yes?"

"What can I do for you?"

"I need flowers."

"Well, we got those." His mouth arches into a condescending smile. "*Any* flowers?"

"No. Not *any* flowers."

Slowly, though visibly, his mug begins to droop, expunging the smile from his face. "What's the occasion?" he asks, facing away from me and trying to disguise an embittered tone.

"It's for a funeral."

"Funeral? ... Tommasini's?"

"Yes."

He scrutinizes me for a moment. "You're cutting it a little close. The wake's today."

"I know. Can you manage?"

"Sure. Do you have anything specific in mind or just something classic?"

"I don't even know what that means ... Can you make something that stands out? Not distasteful though. Here," I hand him a piece of paper with Montanari's name on it.

"What do you want me to write besides the name?" he asks while moving to the desk.

"I don't ... "

"Don't worry. I'll take care of it," he says, waving his hands above his head.

"Tano, Tommasini's ready," Satuzza yells from behind the beads.

"I'll be right there ... Is that all Mr. ... "

"De Angelis."

"Very well, Mr. De Angelis. Is there anything else I can help you with?"

"No, that would be it."

"Excellent! ... Um ... Do you *need* a receipt?"

"Excuse me?"

"No, because ... You know ... I could give you a little ... discount, if you will."

"I'm afraid I need a receipt. Sorry."

"You're sure?"

"It's not up to me."

"Of course. I apologize. Who should I make it out to? Mr. Montanari here? Or ... ?"

"Montanari is fine. I'll pay cash."

"There you go, Mr. De Angelis. Don't you worry about a thing! I'll make it look beautiful."

"Thank you."

I hand him the money, take the receipt, and start for the exit. Though hesitant, I commit to open the door but falter mid-push—my right hand still clutching the door knob, my left foot grazing the sill.

"Did you forget something, Mr. De Angelis?"

"Tommasini ... "

"What about him?"

"He's here, isn't he?"

"Yes. We're about to load him up in the hearse and bring him over to the house. Why? You wanna have a look at him?"

"I don't know … Would that be all right?"

"I don't see why not."

Tano comes around the desk, picks up a little cardboard sign with *'Torno Subito'* written on it, and walks past me.

"Cover your ears," he says, in passing.

I'm not sure what he means by it. Gently, he shuts the glass door and bolts it three times. But the clunking of the lock is so loud and violent it makes the whole front of the shop tremble. My face must be warped in pain, for Tano looks at me and says: "Told you to cover your ears." He hangs the placard right on the glass of the door. "This way," he says, pointing at the beaded curtain.

I follow him.

* * *

"Watch the header," Tano says.

We cross the threshold and enter what reminds me of a sterile operating room. Pale cyan tiles cover the floor and climb halfway up the walls; the upper half is painted off-white. Several metal counters, some empty, the rest covered with meticulously organized instruments, are neatly placed alongside the walls, save for the back where a giant fridge—I assume—looms over the room. In the centre of the ceiling, an industrial-sized light fixture hangs dangerously. One of its fluorescent tubes flickers, making buzzing noises.

"Don't worry. You'll get used to the flickering," he says and approaches the centre of the room, where, over a dressing cot, parallel to a gleaming embalming table perfectly aligned under the light fixture, lies Tommasini's body.

"No need to stand there. You can come closer if you like. You're not afraid, are you?"

"Me? No." I move closer.

"What happened to your leg?"

"What?"

"I noticed you've got a bit of a limp there."

"Oh ... that. It's nothing ... "

"It doesn't look like nothing!"

"I got bitten by a dog. Nothing serious really."

"A dog?"

"Yes."

Tano's features collapse like a snapped rolling shutter, and an air of scepticism descends over his face. Not a word. Not even the semblance of a sound comes out of his mouth —our eyes locked on each other, as though in a staring contest. After a lengthy uncomfortable moment, I'm the one to break the unsettling eyeballing by taking another step forward. As I lean over Tommasini's body, I can still sense Tano's glare on me. A stifling gloomy stillness engulfs the room.

"Well ... " Tano says, with a sudden and unexplained burst of lightheartedness. "You take all the time you need."

"Thanks."

Moving away from Tommasini's body, Tano roves around the room for a while, his body language stiff and tentative. I try not to pay attention, but it's nearly impossible to filter out the irritating scraping of his step. Finally he stops at one of the counters, directly opposite me, and looks about him in search, or so it seems, of something to occupy himself with. His back arches sharply to the left, his face looking downward. He places one hand over the table to support his weight and reaches for something on the floor. It's a transparent container half-filled with some kind of pink substance, which he places on the workbench and begins rearranging some of the equipment already obsessively laid out. He stops for a moment and looks asquint at me.

I tilt my head down to evade his eyes.

Staring directly into Tommasini's face, it strikes me how much more alive, more charismatic he seems than in his photograph. It's as if Tano has given him a personality he never had.

"Mr. Tano," a pubescent voice in the hallway calls out.

"Yes. What is it?"

"Enzo says the hearse is ready."

"All right. Tell him I'll be done in a minute." Tano turns towards me. "Mr. De Angelis, I'm afraid this is all the time we have."

* * *

Other than the building materials, which have been hurriedly removed from the front of the house, and the obituary poster freshly glued on the façade smack in between the door and the window, Tommasini's residence is exactly as I left it three days earlier: windows and doors tightly shut with no visible nor audible human presence inside or outside it, at least from where I'm standing.

I'm pretty certain Tano said he was going to bring the body to the house. I must've arrived here before him. The church bell strikes 12:45. I decide to wait and seek refuge from the sun, which, thanks to a complicit azure sky, is beating down with such force it's melting some of the patched up bituminous surface of the street. There's a balcony with bed sheets and large towels hanging from it a few doors across. Looks like the only place with decent shade in the whole street.

I dash over to it, with both hands interlaced in the shape of a canopy and placed slightly above my sweat-dripping eyebrows to fend off the sun bouncing off car bumpers and windshields. Under the balcony, next to the entrance of the house, there's a tree stump that has been clearly used as a stool—cigarette butts heaped up on the ground to the right, and a gut-churning collage of phlegmy gobs in front of it. I fetch the stump, holding my breath and looking away so as not to retch, and move it as far as possible from the spit within the patch of shade.

I'm about to sit down when I see the hearse pulling up the street. In spite of the blinding sun, I'm able to make out Tano and a young boy sitting next to him. They stop in front of Tommasini's house; the boy swiftly steps off and runs to ring the bell. The door buzzes open. Pushing it enough to peek inside, the boy sticks his head halfway in, has a brief exchange with someone within, judging from the head-bobbing, then rushes to the back of the hearse. Barely a few seconds elapse before the rear doors of the hearse screech wide open to the sides. Tano and three other men, who have just stepped out of Tommasini's house, join the boy. They file behind the hearse.

For a moment or so, all I can see is the occasional see-sawing of the tops of their heads; then, with a chorus of grunts shot out in unison, they reappear from the back of the hearse with a walnut-coloured coffin resting on their shoulders.

After an unintelligible exchange of words, they pivot and head straight to the door, which has been opened wide on both sides by another man, who has now positioned himself in the centre of it so he can manoeuvre the carrying of the casket into the house.

The young boy stays behind, scurrying back and forth to the hearse, unloading some paraphernalia—garlands and other funeral ornaments—onto the curb. As the apprentice offloads the last of the accoutrements, Tano comes back out, followed by two of the three men who helped carry the coffin inside, one of them holding a woven seat, which he places along the wall, a few feet away from the entrance. The two stand on either side of the chair, smoking.

"Anything else?" Tano asks, addressing the boy.

"No, that's it," he replies and without delay darts to the back of the hearse and shuts the doors. Meanwhile, Tano picks up the last few things lying on the curb, and that's when he finally lays eyes on me. He stiffens. The two men also seem to take notice of me. The shutter on the front window of Tommasini's house suddenly rolls up.

 *Chapter Fourteen*

Stealing up the stairs, I'm gradually embraced by a refreshing yet pronounced bouquet of lavender emanating from my room. As I enter, it becomes apparent that not only has Teresa been in here, but that she has cleaned it so punctiliously it sparkles. She has even left on the dresser some flowers in a glass vase with a little hay-tinted card leaning on it. It reads:

> *I took the liberty to tidy up a bit. I hope you*
> *don't mind.*
> *Teresa*

> *P.S. Look in the closet.*

I go to the armoire and open it with some hesitation. She has packed it with a ridiculous number of shirts and suits, all neatly hanging in clear plastic bags—not to mention belts and an array of ties fanned out like fabric swatches.

***

"Oh, there you are! I'm glad you made it. I was about to sit down and have a bite," Teresa says, squirreling about the kitchen. She comes to a sudden halt. "What's the matter?"

"Nothing."

"Then why are you standing there like a post? Have a seat."

I smile and lower myself into a chair and watch her move to and fro between the stove and the table. By the time she sits down, I feel inebriated.

"So," she says, proudly gazing down at the table, which is bursting at the seams with plates, "we have some baked pasta to start, grilled stuffed lamb, a little *caponata* to go with it, and of course cheeses and salami—"

"Who else is coming?"

"Nobody."

"I thought you said a bite."

"What do you mean?"

"Never mind."

"Well, go ahead. Don't be shy."

She gets unusually quiet for a moment and turns away. With a giant serving spoon, she begins piling massive amounts of food on her plate. I must be looking at her funny, however, for she stops in mid-motion.

"What? What is it?" she says, holding in mid-air a spoonful of grease-dripping baked pasta.

I shake my head.

"No, seriously, what?" she reiterates.

"It's nothing really. It's just ... You're so petite, that's all."

"Oh." Her head cocks shyly. "I have a fast metabolism,"

she says, the top of her ears enflamed. "You're not going to eat?"

"No. I mean, yes. I am ... Going to eat."

I take another serving spoon, and, though merely glancing at the steaming hot food makes me sweat through my shirt, I diligently fix myself an abundant plate. She seems pleased. "By the way, I wanted to thank you for tidying up my room and for the clothes up there. You really didn't have to. I can manage without them."

"Nonsense! What use have I got for them anyway? They were my husband's. Do they fit?"

"Like a glove actually."

"Good. Good. Now you can look nice for the wake. You're going, right?"

"Of course."

"I was thinking, maybe we can go together ... to the wake. What do you think? I'm dreading the idea of going with my cousin. He never shuts that big mouth of his. It's a miracle he's still alive ... I'm only joking. I love him. He's ... you know?"

I smile.

Her eyes gleam with expectation.

"Sure. We can go together. No problem."

"Perfect. That's a relief. How's the food? I didn't even ask."

"It's very good. Thank you."

"If you don't mind my asking: I saw you talking to Vannino this morning ... The fruit peddler?"

"Oh yes. He called me over as I was passing by. He wanted to talk to me about something."

"About what?"

"He asked me if I was a relative of yours."

"Oh?" She furrows her brow.

"I had quite an interesting conversation with him, actually. I don't know if you're aware, but he's quite taken with you."

"Who? Vannino? Nooo!"

"I'm serious."

"C'mon. Quit it."

"Why do you think he parks his truck in that particular spot every day?"

"Really?"

She pulls back from me, barely a few degrees, as if to allow herself a moment to let the news sink in. Her pupils flutter, and her lips, slightly ajar, move along with her thoughts. After a handful of seconds, she whips her head back to me with a coquettish smile. She playfully flaps her right hand at me and shakes her head from side to side while bursting into wholehearted, but hysterical, laughter.

* * *

Clad from head to toe in a swath of black chiffon and mazes of passementerie, Teresa is standing by the door, itching to get out of the house. "Oh, there you are!" she says, craning her head a bit. "Are you ready?" I nod. "Well, come down … Let's have a look … Very nice!"

"Thank you. I wasn't sure this tie went with the suit."

"Oh no, it's perfect!"

"You look very nice too," I tell her, not wanting to hurt her feelings.

Blushing, she rushes to the bevelled oval mirror in the

hall tree stand, and with swift, albeit gracious, movements, as though she's been doing this since birth, she pulls a mantilla out of a tiny drawer and puts it on.

We step outside.

Unobstructed, and with no wind to speak of whatsoever, the sun is still beating down with such savagery my clothes are already glued to me by the time we arrive at the main square. Teresa suggests we go to a bar and get a couple of *granite* to freshen up a bit. I don't object. She takes me to a stand-only Lilliputian bar, which is also a tobacconist, lottery dealer, and gift shop. The walls are jammed with stuff crammed on a series of never-ending shelves, erected so high they give the illusion of a remote vanishing point. The vertiginous display coupled with an oversized coffee machine placed on the counter, as opposed to the back wall behind the counter, makes it hard to discern if there's someone tending the bar.

"Ciuzza!" Teresa yells.

Not exactly startled, but somewhat caught off guard, I shoot a glance at her. Her brassy voice doesn't get any gentler when she screams.

"Ciuzza has the best *granita* in town," she says.

"Really?"

"Oh yes. The best. No doubt." Her pupils dilate with excitement.

"Is there someone there?" calls out a distant and echo-y voice coming from somewhere well beyond the counter.

As I lean to look over the coffee machine, I notice—on the back wall, all the way to the right corner—a little brown accordion door, half open. From the opening a mosquito net breathes in and out.

"Ciuzza!" Teresa shouts again.

A hand pulls the net aside. The accordion door slides wide open. Out of it comes a Junoesque lady with piercing dark eyes and woolly black hair neatly pinned up in a low bun, wrapped in what looks like fishnet stockings with a red flower attached to it.

"Teresa, what are you doing here? Is there something wrong?" Ciuzza asks, as she slides out from behind the counter and stoops to kiss Teresa on both cheeks.

"No, no. Nothing's wrong. Knock on wood, eh!"

For a moment, Ciuzza stares at Teresa through dark slits.

"We're going to Tommasini's wake, and I thought we'd grab a couple of *granite* first."

"I see," Ciuzza says. Nodding, she turns toward me. "And who's this?"

"I'm sorry. This is Mr. De Angelis, my lodger."

"Oh, *he*'s the guy!" Ciuzza and Teresa look at each other.

"Pleasure," I say, proffering my hand.

"The pleasure is all mine," Ciuzza says, as she grabs my hand, which she shakes vigorously. An ear-to-ear grin brings a sparkle to her eyes.

"Teresa, can I show you something in the back? It'll just take a minute. You don't mind, Mr. De Angelis, do you?"

"Not at all."

"Be right back," Teresa says and quickly disappears with Ciuzza through the little door.

They don't go too far in though, for I hear them susurrate. I can't quite make out what they are saying, but, judging by their titters, I'm quite sure I'm the subject of whatever it is they are confabulating about. Before long, they come back out, and, between giggles and conspiratorial glances, Ciuzza prepares a couple of *granite* to go for which she won't take any money no matter how much I insist, and, after another round of kisses, Teresa and I are off to the vigil.

* * *

A throng, mostly men, is already gathered in front of Tommasini's house. Detached from the flock, but not too far up the street, a woman runs after a couple of scampering kids, warning them that if they don't stop their father will show them the whip. Once we get closer, the chatting and screaming give way to a leaden silence followed by a soft murmur, which grows louder as we work our way through the crowd. On the other side of the threshold, we find ourselves in a gloomy hallway fully covered on either side with people bobbing their heads as we parade through it. The entrance to the room where Tommasini is being laid out is also congested with people waiting to get in. It's only after the longest ten-minute wait amid whispers, shifty glances, and chronic throat-clearings that we're finally able to enter.

A few steps, and I already have the sensation of donning the burial chamber like a straitjacket. Shrouds of incense streaking out of two large thuribles placed at the foot of the velvet-draped catafalque make it difficult to keep my eyes fully open. I scan the space for a place to stand when Teresa, with a rapid tap on my shoulder and a jerk of her head, draws my attention to a specific corner. By the time I'm able to put things into focus, she's already off to that spot. I follow her. In spite of the dim lighting, she's able to find a nice little niche with a clear view of the entire room, not exactly spacious, and so snug we're actually forced to stand one in front of the other. On the plus side, I have a wall behind me I can lean against.

As my eyes adjust to the dingy setting, I'm able to discern all the faces in the chamber, save for the shadowy figures standing by the wall all the way across. The wavering light of the numerous candles girding the catafalque is too feeble to reach them. Teresa and I are the new fulcrum in the room, given the peculiar mixture of dark slits and gaping eyes aimed our way. Even Tommasini's widow, who's sitting directly opposite us, is unable to disguise, despite a veil of tulle mantling her face, a probing glance.

Soon though, the stares fall away, giving rise to a crescendo of whispers, interrupted solely by the widow's oddly cyclical drawn out sighs, accentuated now and again by truncated bursts of sobbing. Occasionally, I can also hear the slapping of hands on cheeks, necks, and exposed limbs, prompted by the cluster of flies headquartered on Tommasini's face.

The veins of burning myrrh, which rows of women, doggedly fanning themselves, turn into fine mist, and the palpable humidity, not to mention the questionable personal hygiene of some of the mourners, are to blame for the lack of breathable air. To make things worse, the room temperature has now reached a febrile state. The feeling is like being inside some sort of living organism: The heat radiates with ever-rising pressure from body to body as it does through connecting tissues.

A door across the room, until now hidden because of all the people standing in front of it, whines open enough to let in a wedge of pale-yellow light. A concerto of creaky chairs, accompanied by an almost choreographed turning of necks, follows. The door opens wider, revealing two silhouettes: a woman holding hands with a little girl. As they step inside and walk through a human corridor, the child breaks free and makes a run for the catafalque, stopping quite suddenly by the censer on the left side of it. She's sombrely dressed far beyond her age, yet seemly. Her chestnut hip-long hair, held back with a black velvet band, softly cascades along her slender contours. She stands in absolute stillness, looking down at Tommasini. The woman who ushered her in catches up with her and tries unsuccessfully to whisk her away.

"Marinella," the widow says in a broken, anemic tone, extending her arm.

The child untangles herself from the woman, rushes to her mother and climbs onto her lap, gently letting her head find comfort on her mother's bosom. The woman, after a brief exchange of glances with the widow, reluctantly moves away from the catafalque and disappears behind the shadowy figures.

At that moment, the little girl gets off her mother's lap just as quickly as she got on and moves close to Tommasini's body. The widow leans forward to stop the child but gives up in mid-motion. The girl is standing by her father's face, waving her hand over it to disperse the cluster of flies feasting on it. Then, all of a sudden, the child aims her large almond-shaped eyes—of a striking aquamarine colour—in my direction. And even though I'm well aware it's impossible for her to see my face where I'm standing, at least not fully, she seems to be staring right at me. Feeling faint, I lean against the wall. I close my eyes to stop the room and the distorted faces of the mourners from swirling. Droplets of cold sweat stream down my temples. I reach for the handkerchief in my right pocket and zigzag it across my face.

"You all right?" Teresa whispers.

"It's a little hot in here, that's all."

"Don't worry. We're leaving soon."

I nod.

Chapter Fifteen

"**D**o you mind going back by yourself?" I ask Teresa, as we come out of Tommasini's house.

"Sure. You all right?"

"I need to take a walk."

"Still not feeling good, huh?"

"I'm okay. I need some air, that's all." Sensing a little disappointment, I quickly add: "But I can accompany you first if you like."

"No, no, no, there's no need for that. You know, I might be petite, but I can still take care of myself ... I'm joking."

"I know."

"Well ... I guess I'll be off." She makes as if to leave.

"Wait! I feel like I'm being rude. Why don't you let me walk you home?"

"No. Don't be silly. I have to make a stop anyway."

"You positive?"

"Absolutely." And without adding another word, she

starts off down the street with short, yet brisk, steps. About to turn the corner, she halts and swivels back, like a little girl pirouetting in front of a mirror. "You coming back for dinner?" she shouts.

"Sure."

"Nine-ish." And after another sharp whirl, she marches out of sight, the hammering of her heels lagging behind.

There's no one left in front of Tommasini's house. Only the chair and a few ashtrays overflowing with cigarette butts remain. The whole neighbourhood has seemingly fallen back into a deep slumber, but a gentle wind pregnant with aromas redolent of supper suggests otherwise.

For a time, I stake out the house from across the street. A whole twenty minutes wears on, and not a single soul has either gone in or come out. While standing there, sweating profusely, I detect the figure of a woman behind a see-through lace curtain on a balcony facing me. I observe her, trying to avoid direct eye contact. She's definitely spying on me. I try to ignore her, but I can't. Getting increasingly restive, I decide to leave.

At first, I stride purposefully down the street, forcing myself to look straight ahead. Nearing the main square, however, I begin to vacillate. The closer I get, the more I have to push myself to move forward. Eventually, I'm not able to take another step. It's as though I've been pushing the rubber of a giant slingshot that has now reached its maximum draw, and I'm about to be shot out.

I rush back to Tommasini's house.

I search for the lady on the balcony. It looks like she's gone. In any case, I hunt for another spot a bit more discreet and end up wedging myself between two parked cars.

It's not exactly comfortable, but at least it shields me from wandering eyes.

* * *

"Marinella, don't go too far! ... You hear me?" a shrill feminine voice shouts.

From between the two cars, I look out without risking being exposed. Two ladies with grotesquely round bellies stand outside Tommasini's house. Both robed in black and wearing shawls—one over her head, the other one over her shoulders, the ladies are smoking and whispering to each other. Now and again, they throw a fleeting glance at Marinella, Tommasini's daughter, who's off to the same side where the chair is.

The little girl is slowly walking in front of the house, aligning one foot in front of the other as if tracking an imaginary line; her right hand runs along the wall; her eyes gaze downward. As she reaches the chair, she climbs on it and folds her arms around her drawn up knees.

"Marinella, get down!" one of the ladies yells.

Marinella ignores her.

Amid grunts of displeasure, the two ladies with a series of quick, short puffs finish smoking, throw the cigarette butts to the ground, and almost in unison cry: "Marinella, let's go."

The child doesn't budge.

Visibly frustrated by Marinella's defiance, the ladies march toward her. They try, in vain, to persuade her to get back in the house. It's only after the child lets out a glass-shattering scream, so acute, that the ladies recoil.

"All right, another ten minutes ... Yes?" the lady with shawl over her head says. The little girl doesn't react. "You stay here, though. Don't go anywhere."

Again, Marinella doesn't say anything.

Resigned, the two ladies willy-nilly make their way through the threshold, shaking their heads and murmuring something unintelligible.

Meanwhile, Marinella hasn't moved—her hands still wrapped around her legs, her chin rested on her knees, her eyes staring off into the distance.

I peek at the door. The ladies have disappeared into the hall. There's no one coming out of it, no one standing on the doorsill, and, as far as I can discern, no one immediately beyond it, although the corridor is way too dingy to be certain of it. All I can see is a deep black mass, so rich and uniform it's hard to imagine existence beyond it. Were it not for the little girl curled-up on the chair, I'd think the burial chamber, Tommasini, the mourners, the widow, Teresa, the shadowy figures were merely figments of my imagination.

I check the windows and balconies in front of me, and as far to the sides as I can distinguish, for any unwelcome peeping. I can't see any. I wait a touch longer, however, before I charily slide out from between the two cars. Still hunched and slightly squatted so as not to be seen, I edge alongside the automobile to my left while keeping an eye on Marinella through the car's windows.

Except for a barely perceptible rocking, she hasn't moved. I stay behind the car, hunkered down, unseen. Suddenly, my skin stings like a tight and painfully itchy wool undergarment. As a reflex, I straighten up and come out from behind the car. I stand there, hardly a few degrees off from a direct eye-line with the little girl, somewhat unhinged. The view: unobstructed. No cars, no blinds, no beaded curtains, nothing.

She sees me. No room for doubt this time. She's staring right at me.

Just then, what starts in the guise of an innocuous fidget down in my legs, a twitch, an involuntary shudder, grows swiftly into a bone-deep tremor, rising and propagating through the whole of my body, reaching the most recondite crevices within it. From the top of my skull to the very tip of my digits, I can feel the aftershocks.

Though struggling to gain any measure of control, I manage, however tentatively, to take a step forward, then another, and another, and before I can even realize it I'm walking steadily toward her. She seems unfazed. In fact, she hasn't stirred, her piercing eyes firmly locked on mine. At about two to three paces from her, I have to stop. Her gaze is so daunting it's debilitating. Every skeletal muscle in my body stiffens to the extent of unresponsiveness. Even my lungs seem to have gotten tighter, letting in but shallow and short breaths, enough to prevent me from folding down to ground. I remain there immobile—as if under a bell jar. I can see her; I can smell her. Yet, in the manner of sleep paralysis, I'm unable to move.

Not until a woman's voice, without the least warning, calls out the little girl's name that I'm heaved out of this cocooned, quasi-paralytic state. Her voice ruptures the dense silence like a startling crow's caw. My surroundings, as though suddenly subjected to a different gravitational pull, come crushing down on me. Somewhat dazed, I search for the voice. A black-clad wrinkly old woman with goat's eyes, chin hair, and a sizeable moustache stands on the doorsill, her upper body slantwise, looking at us. The seams nesting her face are so deep and asymmetrical they form odd geometrical shapes.

"Marinella," she cries out again and, with an almost dreamlike slowness, lowers herself to the ground.

The little girl pays no heed whatsoever to her. She doesn't even dignify her with the fleetest of glances. The old lady, now on the ground, walks, with the help of a cane, along the wall toward Marinella, spewing out all sorts of inscrutable sounds. Reaching the little girl, the old lady grabs her arm and tries to yank her off the chair. But Marinella won't have it; she resists it with all her might. The back-and-forth between the two of them escalates fairly quickly into senseless, if not farcical, tugging. Marinella puts an end to it with another heart-stopping scream. The old lady cringes away, exposing her putrefied teeth.

"What the hell is going on here?" shouts a husky man with woolly hair, standing on the doorstep. The old lady spouts something in tight vernacular I can't understand. "Mom, calm down," the man says, getting close to them. But the old lady, even more stubborn than the little girl, ignores him and launches into a tirade. "*Gesù*, Giuseppe, *e* Maria! Mom, what did I just say?" he scolds. The old lady, noticeably wounded and finally out of words, sets off to the house

Marinella jumps off the chair and hurries to the man. She latches on to him, as if seeking to be rescued.

"What's the matter? Why are you upsetting grandma? … This is not the time for tantrums." The child tightens her grip and sinks her face into his abdomen. "I know ... I know," he says, folding his left arm around Marinella's figure and gently stroking her hair with his right hand. "It's okay. Forget about it."

As though noticing my presence for the first time, he gives me a sidelong once-over. "Who are *you*?" he asks, his tone less than kind. And without even waiting for an answer, he adds: "Please, forgive me." He's looking at me straight in the face now. "I didn't mean to be rude ... My mom can be worse than a child sometimes."

I proffer a sympathetic smile. He reciprocates and presses on fondling Marinella's hair.

"I saw you inside earlier. You came in with Teresa Giuffrè, right?" I nod. "You're not from around here. You a relative or something?"

"No, no." Noticing his brow crease and his eyes shrink a touch, I add: "I'm here on business."

"Business? Here? In Figallia? ... In this godforsaken place? I can't even begin to imagine ... Wait a second. What's your name?"

"It was me—" The man interrupts me with a quick, and somewhat brusque, hand gesture.

"Marinella ... Be a good girl, go back inside. Would you do that for your uncle, Alfio? Yes?"

The little girl untangles herself from her uncle. Though subtle, I can tell she's been peering at me. He gives her a big kiss on her forehead. Marinella takes off. We watch her walk, climb the step, cross the threshold, and leap inevitably out of sight. Instantly, Alfio flips his large figure over to me and gets closer. So close actually, I can count his nose hairs.

"You got some balls showing your face here, you know that?" he spurts out.

"What do you mean?"

"What do I *mean*? What do *you* mean?"

"Look … I commiserate with you … I'm painfully aware Peppe—"

"Don't you dare say his name!"

"I know he was waiting for me at the station when it happened … But it was an accident, wasn't it?"

"An *accident*? … Right."

I lower my voice to a whisper. "Listen, we had no idea—"

"I'm gonna tell you this once, so you better listen good. Do not show your face here again, and do *not* come to the funeral tomorrow. Understood?" I make as if to say something, but Alfio blocks me: "Shut your mouth and get the hell away before I tear you limb from limb."

Chapter Sixteen

I pace around the village for a while, sticking to the less populous parts: from the belvedere all the way to the wall shrine — long-forgotten considering the poor state it's in — atop the village. I don't even know how many times I walk the same streets. Eventually, my ceaseless wandering attracts the curious: prying eyes creep up behind slit blinds, mosquito nets, penumbras. I try to ignore them for as long as I can, but the sheer number of stares becomes asphyxiating and forces me to change course.

By mere chance, I find myself walking toward the lodging. As I turn onto *Via* Cavour, I spot Vannino. It looks like he's wrapping up for the day, rolling down the tarpaulin at the rear of his truck. His movements are assured and remarkably precise, yet nonchalant. I watch him tighten the tarpaulin to the flatbed, give a firm tug to the rope keeping it in place, go round the truck, climb inside the cab, and in less than a minute take off, leaving behind a thick cloud of burnt gasoline.

I walk to the lodging.

The key to the front door has slid inside the deadbolt. But I have no recollection of this action ever taking place. Though banal, the apparent triviality of it is unnerving. I'm holding the key between my thumb and index finger. I didn't realize I was holding it with such a tight grip, not until I thought about it. The unexpected frustration leaves me standing, weighing whether or not to give the key a turn—a simple enough decision, which has strangely taken on a much weightier mental process.

The sole idea of having to small talk or to be subjected to a torrent of banalities, the hallmark of Teresa's repertoire, is both irritating and comforting. I'm about to give the key in the padlock a twist when, overcome by a sudden repulsion, I withdraw it and hastily walk away, veering off at the first corner.

Despite the soreness in my leg, I move fast, covering—without a moment's thought, as though driven in *toto* by sense memory—familiar grounds. I inevitably, it seems to me, arrive at the main square, which is infested with flocks of villagers, Vespas, and street vendors. My first instinct is to turn around. Instead, I stand there still in the middle of the road, same as an oblivious, awestruck tourist. All of a sudden, a car horn reminiscent of a mariachi-band tune blasts to my left. I turn around. One look at the driver and it's clear to me there is no use wasting my breath on him. He flaunts a ludicrous perm and a pencil moustache, his hands mantled with rings. His vehicle—obviously not a sports car but dressed-up like one: spoilers, shiny spokes, decals—looks even more ridiculous than he does. I move out of the way.

Carefully avoiding eye contact so as not to be drawn into conversation, I start circling the plaza. I must've lowered my guard, however, for an African migrant, accompanied by a revolting stench, manages to sneak up on me, almost cutting me off. He barks something right to my face. Because of his pronounced north-African accent, the handful of chopped-up Italian-Sicilian words he's picked up come out of his mouth with rapid, violent bursts. He's wearing a frayed, brown fine-patterned wool suit, including a vest. On his right shoulder, he carries a thick stack of rugs; on the other, a slew of scarves. His forearms are covered with all kinds of necklaces and wristbands.

"*Amico*," he says, pointing at the rugs. I shake my head. "*Aspet, aspet* ... " He quickly raises his arms to better show me the trinkets. "*Cinque mila.*" I shake my head again, this time waving my hand as well. "*Tu amico ... quanto dare?*" I'm starting to get really annoyed with him. I make as if to pull away, but he puts his left hand on my shoulder. I shoot him a look. "*Amico, amico* ... "

"Stop calling me *amico*, okay?"

"*Scusa! ... Non ti arrabbiare* ... " Just when I think he finally got it, I see him reaching for the right side of his jacket and pulling it open. Attached to it on the inside, he's got a black cloth with an array of knockoff watches on display.

"Maybe I'm not explaining myself. I don't want anything. Is that clear? ... I don't want a necklace, I don't want a watch, and certainly I don't want a goddam rug!"

A morbid silence follows.

I look about me. All I can see is a parade of paralyzed stares. Another migrant from across the street, standing next to a handcart with all kinds of junk on it for sale, shouts something in Arabic. The one in front of me yells something in return, also in Arabic. Then he backs off and steps away amid murmurs. Although the villagers in the piazza appear to have gone back to minding their own business, I can't help but feeling conspicuous, so I think it best to seek shelter somewhere more private. A restaurant, give or take, a block further up draws my attention. It's the same one I was trapped in during the storm.

* * *

The restaurant's lights are entirely dimmed down, and there's no one in sight.

"Hello! ... Hello! Anybody here?" No answer.

I'm about to turn around when I hear a woman's voice call: "Who's there?" It's the owner's voice, I think. As soon as she steps out of the shadow, I recognize her. I see her, but I don't think she can see me, at least not well, because of the bright backlight coming from the windows behind me. Chances are, I'm barely a silhouette to her right now. "Who is it?" she asks, coming toward me.

"It's De Angelis."

"Who?" I meet her halfway. "But of course, Mr. De Angelis, I remember you. Sorry, I didn't recognize you right away, but I couldn't see well, you know ... Anyway, what can I do for you?"

"This is probably a stupid question, but ... are you open?"

"Oh ... No. Not yet. Why?"

"Is it all right if I sit here? My leg is a bit sore."

She hesitates answering. "Sure ... I don't see why not. Take a seat wherever you like ... Um ... I have to go in the back though. I still have some prep to finish."

"Please, don't mind me. I'm just going to rest a while."

"No problem. Stay as long as you like," she says, her tone registering as sincere. "Well," she carries on, commencing a sentence she merely finishes with a sweeping, albeit awkward, hand gesture. A signal I interpret as make yourself at home, or something along those lines. With her arm still held up in the air, for no apparent reason, she lingers a trice longer. And no sooner a faint smile gathers at the corners of her mouth than she swings back into the shadows.

I lift a chair and carry it to the window where the jukebox and pay phone are. I place the chair under the window and push it right up to the large glass giving on to the square. I sit there, looking out. An influx of townspeople, coming from the surrounding streets, floods the already crowded piazza. Even the number of vehicles — parked, double-parked, and obsessively circling around — grows exponentially, along with the noise level. And though I'm viewing all this through a fairly thick sheet of glass, it isn't enough to muffle the blowing of car horns and the mounting clamour.

The hubbub, however, doesn't last long, for the sun, almost without a moment's notice, disappears and so do most of the locals. In the span of half-hour, there's nearly no one in the square but a scattering of bar habitués and devout churchgoers.

As darkness forcefully moves in, I realize the restaurant's floodlights above the storefront have been switched on. I look at the dining room. The wall fixtures have also been turned on. They give off a soft, warm glow, as though purposefully designed to mask the many scuffs, rips, cracks, grease and humidity stains marring the long-decaying establishment.

I hear men's voices trickle in from somewhere outside, close enough to the restaurant I'm able to make out what they're saying. They're arguing about a football game. And just when the back and forth among them grows louder, the restaurant's front door chimes open. A couple of men wearing summer suits—one solid grey, the other one tan with a subtle pattern—come dawdling in still quibbling about the game. The one in the grey suit, also the taller and leaner of the two, goes on and on about an unfair, according to him but vividly disputed by the other man, last-minute goal ruled out.

The two stop arguing the moment they take notice of me. "*Bonasera*," they say, echoing each other. Their heads slightly bow down, as if in reverence. I reciprocate.

"Good evening," the lady says, having stepped in the dining room. Exuberant, she trots to the door to greet them. Only after a tad drawn-out exchange of pleasantries do they walk away from the entrance, in the direction of the bar. Once there, the wispy lady excuses herself. Leaning on the counter, the two men resume talking about the game, picking up the conversation exactly where they left off: the ruled-out goal. The shorter one takes the lead this time. "I'm telling you. The striker was offside."

"No, he was not!" the taller one blurts out. "How could you not see it? Huh? Well ... I guess ... There are at least two reasons I can think of!"

"Oh? What's that? Why don't you enlighten me?"

"You're either as blind as the referee or—"

"Or what?"

"Never mind."

"No, no, no. Finish that sentence if you got any balls!"

"If *I* got any balls? ... I gotta tell you, that's priceless ... *If I got any balls* ... You're the one to talk ... Farinelli over here!"

"What'd you call me?"

"Forget it."

"That's right, forget it. You lost this one. Admit it."

"I don't gotta admit nothing. I didn't loose nothing—"

"You know perfectly well he was offside."

"Sure, maybe a lock of his hair was offside."

"What's that? Comedy?"

"Calm down you two," a man, in his forties, coming from the back of the restaurant says. He's short but athletic, with hair neatly slicked back, and wearing a server's uniform.

"Whoa, look who's here!" the shorter of the two men says.

"Vicè ... What happened? When did they let you out?" the taller one says, teasing.

"What? No more room in jail or something?" the shorter man says.

"That's funny. Very funny," the server says, twining through the dining room tables for final touches. "Wait a second ... What are you two doing here? Shouldn't you be out there mugging old ladies? ... I don't know ... Stealing the change from the charity box at the church or something?"

"If I didn't know better," the taller man says, "I think Vicè here is calling us petty thieves."

"No, he wouldn't do that, would he?" the short one says. "Would you, Vicè?"

"*Minchia*! Don't you ever get tired of listening to yourselves blabber?" The server sidles behind the bar. "What can I get you, you low life?"

"Two *Biancosarti* on the rocks," the tall one calls out.

"*Biancosarti*? *Minchia*, you guys play rough! Where'd you leave your skirts?"

"Enough with that, huh?" the one in the tan suit says, visibly irritated.

"What? Did I touch a nerve?"

"Come on! He's right. Enough is enough."

"You know," the server says. "I haven't been to the bathroom in a couple of days. Do me a favour. Why don't you keep talking? Your voice, I don't know, there's something laxative about it."

"Stop breaking balls!" the tall one says.

Slowly leaning forward, the server says: "Balls? ... Like you know anything about balls—"

"*Piezz e merd*—"

"What's going on here?" the lady, having rushed into the room, says.

They all recoil.

"Nothing," the server says, breaking the tense moment. "We're just kidding around here." And looking at the two men, he goes on to say: "Don't be so sensitive. Jesus Christ! How about a round of drinks on the house?" The two men nod. "And one for the gentleman in the corner over there." He pours the drinks for the two at the bar. "What can I get you, mister?"

"Who, me?" I say, without thinking.

"Who else? Unless you know something we don't, you're the only one here." They all laugh, including the owner, although she tries to hide it, out of politeness, I suppose.

"Yes, I guess I deserve that, don't I? That was a pretty stupid thing to say."

The lady doesn't seem to be able to hold it anymore. A big smile broadens her face.

"Nah, don't beat yourself up, it happens. We're all bound to say something stupid sooner or later," the server says. "But I can tell you're not like certain people I know." He points with the tilt of his head at the two men. "They got a gift for it."

"Vicè, enough already!" the two men cry out at the same time. Even the owner warns him to cut it out and quickly steps out of the dining room.

"All right, all right ... I swear to God that was the last one." The server crosses his index fingers, brings them to his mouth, and like a kid gives them two big sonorous kisses. "Happy?" Both men give him the finger. "So ... What's your drink, mister?"

"It's all right."

"I insist."

"Come on, don't be shy. Come drink with us," the man in the grey suit says.

Not to make a big deal out of it, I get up and walk to the bar. "I guess I can have some cognac, if you have."

"Cognac? An aristocrat! ... Let's see ... I'm afraid I don't have any. Vecchia Romagna okay?"

"Sure."

He pours me a drink, another one for himself, and raises his up in the air. The two men and I follow suit.

* * *

To my surprise, in less than hour, the restaurant fills up with locals. I guess the food must be a draw, certainly not the ambiance or the hideous decor. The two men and I are sitting at a table in the back by the kitchen, drinking a carafe of red wine. I tried to keep to myself, but they wouldn't have it. Something about no one should ever eat alone. Amazingly, the two are still arguing about the game. At one point they even try to involve me in the conversation. Thankfully, I'm able to deflect it by claiming no interest in sports whatsoever. They seem shocked at first, but they get over it fairly quickly.

Vicè, the server, who's also a relative of the owner apparently, is busy taking orders. He manages, however, to stop by every so often. And each time, he doesn't miss a chance to make a crack about the two men sitting with me, angering them no end. The two clowns are easy targets, and the server really seems to get a kick out of it. And the angrier they get, the more he sticks it to them. I actually feel bad for the two simpletons.

"All right, here we go," the owner says, showing up with our food. "Three rabbits, extra large. I don't know why, but I'm feeling generous today. You two" — addressing my dinner companions — "don't get used to it ... Well ... *Bon appetito*!" And with a big smile that makes her eyes twinkle, she darts back to the kitchen.

The two men waste no time and throw themselves at the food, as if famished. They practically inhale it and pick through the bones like scavengers. They don't even bother wiping their mouths, which have reddened with sauce and collected bits of shredded meat. They are almost through with their food, and I haven't even started with mine yet. I gaze down at my plate—trying not to think about the barbaric, bordering on nauseating, scene unfolding before my eyes—and take a stab at it.

The meat itself is pretty tender, but the tomato sauce is so thick and oily that it has turned orange. A few bites and I can already feel my intestinal walls getting coated with grease, and no amount of water can wash it off. I have no choice but to resort to wine; its acidity is the only thing that cuts through it. By the end of the meal, I'm inebriated.

* * *

The rush has petered out, and the restaurant is nearly empty now. Aside from a couple of tables at the opposite side of the dining room getting ready to leave, ours is the last one remaining. The owner has joined us, and so has Vicè, who's also brought another carafe of wine. Bringing more alcohol to the table strikes me as a bad idea, the two men being quite rowdy already.

"So, you haven't told us what you're doing in this shithole," Vicè says. "I'm sorry, what's your name again?"

"De Angelis."

"Oh, right. So, what brings you to our beautiful Figallia?" he asks again. And looking at the two men, he goes on to say: "Not the view, obviously."

He camouflages this nth caustic remark with in innocuous grin, but I can tell he's really revelling in it. Even the owner is unable to hold back a short but explosive laugh. To be fair, neither of the two men is exactly an Adonis, far from it. The two idiots take this latest insult quite well. They barely shake their heads. Perhaps the numerous glasses of wine they've washed down are starting to take their toll.

"So ... Are you gonna make me ask again?"

"What?"

"What! He says! What am I speaking in tongues here? *Minchia*, how much wine did you drink?"

"Some."

"Some? ... From where I'm standing, I'd say it's definitely more than some."

"Leave the gentlemen alone," the owner says.

"I'm kidding. He knows it's all in good fun ... Don't you?"

I nod.

"So ... *Minchia*, I have to say, I'm starting to feel a little redundant on my part!"

"*Redundant*," the two men echo, fake bowing in respect. "Someone has finally cracked a book!" the taller one says.

"That's right. Unlike you, you lowlife illiterates! ... Anyway, what was I saying? ... You know what? I could care less. There. I said it!" He pours himself a brimming glass of wine and downs it in one gulp.

"Slow down, you ... " the owner says.

"I'm here on business," I tell him so as to put an end to whatever this is.

"Then you *can* speak! ... What kind of business?"

"Vicè!" the owner says.

"What? It's just a question, for Chrissakes! He doesn't have to answer it if he doesn't want to."

With a hand gesture trailed by a headshake, I let the owner know I don't have a problem with it. "Nothing important. A little real estate thing."

"How'd it go? Good?" Vicè asks.

"No. Unfortunately, not worth coming all the way down here from Milan, I'm afraid. No offence."

They all wave understanding.

"What are you gonna do? Right?" Vicè fetches the carafe of wine and tops up everybody's glass. "You win some, you lose some ... "

The owner and the two men bob their heads in agreement. Vicè raises his glass. "To better times. *Cin Cin*!"

We all raise our glasses and robotically repeat: "To better times."

"You all right?" the owner asks. "Forgive me for saying it, but you don't look so good all of a sudden."

"Maybe, a little too much wine," I respond, downplaying the level of my inebriety.

She gets up, goes to the bar, and briefly disappears behind the counter. She re-emerges holding a couple of bottles of mineral water. After pouring some for everybody at the table, she sits back down. I thank her.

"You going to the funeral tomorrow?" Vicè asks, addressing the two men.

"Yes," the man in the tan suit answers, while the one in the grey suit simply nods. "You?"

"Of course."

"What a shame," the owner says.

"Funeral?" I say, pretending not to know anything about it.

They all go quiet and eye each other.

"Nothing," Vicè says, breaking the silence. "It's this local guy who had an accident."

"What kind of accident?" I ask.

They exchange glances again.

"I suppose it's all right," Vicè says. "He was shot to death. Looks like he caught a bullet that wasn't meant for him. Talk about bad luck, huh?"

I refrain from commenting.

"He was such a nice man," the owner says. "He leaves behind a wife and a little girl. How tragic is that?"

"She's such a beautiful lady too!" the man in the grey suit says.

"Very true," the short one says.

"What's the matter with you two? What's that got to do with anything?" the owner says.

"No ... We're just saying here, that's all," the man in the grey suit says. The owner bounces to her feet and storms out of the dining room. "What? What did I say?"

Vicè signals him to drop it. "That poor little girl. Growing up without a father. I can't even begin to imagine what that's like. Especially at that age. What is she? Ten? Eleven?"

"Eleven," the man in the tan suit says.

"How do you know?" Vicè asks, pouncing on the opportunity to make another crack. "Is there something you wanna tell us?"

Picking up on Vicè's intention, the man in the grey suit piles it on: "That's right. How do you know?"

"My mom told me, you assholes! Stop breaking my balls, both of you."

"Anyway," Vicè says with a devious smirk. "She's such a beautiful girl too. She takes after her mother, obviously."

"I think she's even prettier," the man in the grey suit says.

"Absolutely," the other says. "Those eyes!"

"Enough!" I cry out. They freeze. "She's only a little girl. Aren't you ashamed of yourselves!" The words spurt out of my mouth uncontrollably.

"Are you looking at me?" the man in the tan suit says, standing up, his index finger menacingly aimed at me.

"Don't you dare point!"

"Whoa, whoa, whoa ... What's going on here?" Vicè says, holding out his hands in a placating manner. "Everybody, calm down. Take a deep breath. You" — to the man in the tan suit — "sit down. And you" — addressing me this time — "What the hell happened? ... He's an idiot, you know. He talks to talk. That's all. You gotta take it easy!"

"I'm sorry, I didn't mean to ... I apologize, okay?" He gives me a tentative nod, as a way of accepting my apology.

"All right, let's all have a drink," Vicè says.

It's no use. Even after Vicè finishes pouring the wine, we all sit there in silence. At one point, it gets so dead still I can hear the hum of the appliances from the kitchen.

Chapter Seventeen

I'm awoken by the clanking of pots and pans. I must've
blacked out, for I find myself lying on a sofa inside a tiny
office, which I assume is still in the restaurant. There's no
window in the office. The little light that's spilling in comes
from the half-opened door. The room reeks, but I'm not
sure of what. All I know is that it's a pungent smell.

I get up and walk to the kitchen, thinking I'm going
to find the owner there. Instead, it's the veiny kitchen helper I first saw when stranded here during the storm. I un-
intentionally startle her.

"Sorry, I didn't mean to catch you off guard."

"No, no, it's all right. *Bongiorno.*"

"Is the owner here?"

"No. Not yet. She won't be in till later. Why?"

"Did she say anything to you?"

"That you were in the office, sleeping it off. That's all
… Oh, I almost forgot. She left a message for you … On
the door."

"Thank you."

And there it is: an envelope with my name on it taped on the glass door. I open it:

> *Mr. De Angelis,*
>
> *I hope you're feeling better. We didn't know where you were staying, so after you blacked out we put you in the office. I don't know how much you remember of what went on last night. Anyway, without going into details, let's just say that we wouldn't want a repeat of that. So, please don't take this the wrong way, but I would like you to not come back to my restaurant. I'm aware this might sound a little harsh, but I really believe this is for the best. I'm confident you'll understand. Thanks.*

* * *

At the lodging, I try to sneak upstairs, but Teresa ambushes me in the hallway.

"Where have you been?" I stop in mid-stride. "I was waiting for you last night, but you never showed up ... I was actually worried. I almost sent my cousin looking for you."

"I'm sorry. I completely forgot."

"You forgot?"

"Not exactly ... I stopped at this restaurant to rest my leg a little. Then one thing led to another, and I ended up staying for dinner. And I guess I had quite a few drinks ... "

"I see."

"I didn't mean to be disrespectful."

"You could've called!"

Out of excuses, I nod. "I don't mean to be rude, but I really need to take a shower—"

"What happened to your face?"

"My face? What do you mean?"

"You got something on your right cheek. Did someone punch you?"

I'm not sure what to say. I bring my right hand to my cheek, and as soon as I touch it I can feel a sharp sting. "Um ... You really need to excuse me now."

"Sure, of course. Don't let me keep you."

I rush up to my room, bolt the door, and go to the mirror. My right cheek and jaw have visible livid bruises. I check my hands. The knuckles in my right hand are a bit reddened and swollen as well. The strangest thing is I can't remember what the hell happened. The whole night is a blur.

I slowly get undressed and hop in the shower.

* * *

"Feeling better?" Teresa asks as I enter the kitchen. She's sitting at the table working on her centrepiece. I can tell she's trying to move past last night's events, but despite her best efforts her voice betrays a lingering disappointment.

"Please allow me to apologize again. I really didn't mean any disrespect. You were kind enough to invite me to dinner, and I should've been here. No excuse. It was very rude of me."

She seems to soften a bit. "Don't worry about it. It's all

in the past already." Drawing attention to the bruises on my face, she goes on to say: "It looks like you had a rough night though. What happened? If you don't mind my asking."

"I know this is going to sound strange, but I have no recollection whatsoever."

"Did you get in a fight or something?"

"As I said, I'm not sure. I know there was quite a bit of drinking, but other than that I really don't ... Anyway, I'd rather not talk about it."

"Oh, I'm sorry. I didn't mean to pry."

"It's quite all right."

"I don't suppose you're hungry. You must feel pretty hungover still. Perhaps, some coffee?"

"Thank you."

She throws the tambour on the table, jumps to her feet, and carries on to make the coffee. "You still going to the funeral though, right?"

"Yes. That's soon, no?"

"About an hour. If it's all right with you, we can go together."

"Sure. I'd like that ... Shit!"

"What's wrong? Does it hurt?"

"What? ... No ... It's not that ... My follow up injections. I almost forgot. I can't skip it."

"Is it today?"

"Yes."

"So, what's the problem? We can stop at the Doctor's on the way. No?"

"I suppose we could, yes. Well, we should probably get a move on. After the coffee, I'll get changed. I saw a dark suit in the closet."

"Oh yes, the charcoal one … My husband loved that suit."

"If you prefer, I can wear something else."

"What? No … Why? There's no reason for that. Besides, that's the only dark suit."

"If you're sure?"

She's about to say something but instead flaps her hands in the air. I let it be. Right after the coffee, I go upstairs and change into the dark suit. Even this one fits like a glove. By the time I come back down, Teresa is waiting for me at the door. It's hard to believe she's wearing even more chiffon and passementeries than yesterday.

"Ready?" she asks.

I nod. "You?"

She opens her arms and slowly makes a full turn. "What do you think?"

We set off to the Doctor's office to get my second shot, which for some reason is even more painful than the first one, and then head to the church for the funeral mass.

* * *

From afar, I can already detect large crowds of townspeople streaming into the square. It looks like the whole town is attending the funeral. Teresa and I make our way through the people into the church.

"I'm afraid we're not going to find any seats," she remarks.

It turns out, she's right. The basilica is packed to the rafters. There's barely any room left in the three-tier loggia.

But somehow, Teresa, with me in tow, manages to squeeze through and finds some standing room by one of the columns close to the altar.

"I think this is as close as we're gonna get," she says.

"Honestly, I didn't think we would get this far in."

She flaunts a complacent smile. I let her bask in it.

The inside of the Basilica—a stunning example of Arab-Norman architecture, with glittering-gold mosaics, and intricate wooden *muqarnas* ceiling—is even more ostentatious than its exterior. The austere elongated figures depicted along the walls and the central apse look down on us with admonishment.

There seems to be some kind of commotion by the narthex. It must be the arrival of the casket, for the people crowding the entryway quickly part in the middle. I can see the coffin now escorted into the nave, being raised up, and solemnly advance toward the altar, where a bier has been erected. On either side of the catafalque, rows of garlands are stacked up so high it makes me wonder from where the priest is going to celebrate mass. I don't see either a pulpit or a lectern on either side of the altar, as one would expect.

Alfio, Tommasini's brother-in-law, is one of the pallbearers. He's right in front on the side of the coffin facing Teresa and me. As they pass through, I catch him glancing over in our direction. Though a fleeting glance, and in spite of the sea of funeral attendees all around me, I have the impression he spotted me. The chief mourners, Peppe's immediate family, are behind the coffin, and, like it, proceed gravely. I don't see Marinella among them, though. There's another kid, but definitely not Marinella. I scan the whole church to locate her. Nothing. Perhaps she was too upset to come to the funeral. Come to think of it, at the wake she did seem to have taken her father's death particularly hard.

As soon as the casket is lowered onto the bier, Peppe's family and relatives split and file along the two front pews and take a seat; the rest of the mourners follow suit. The incessant chattering tapers off. Save for the occasional whisper, only the coughing of chain-smokers and the chronic throat clearings reverberate in the many vaults of the church. All the windows and doors have been shut, and the light fixtures above the congregation have been dimmed almost all the way down, directing everyone's attention to the now, by contrast, extremely bright altar. The light hitting the gold mosaics covering the chancel's walls spills back onto the nave, softened, nearly dispersed by shrouds of burning myrrh, suffusing the mourners.

Before long, a couple of church volunteers wheel in a squeaky platform with a lectern on it and place it on the left side of the main tier between the altar and the front pews. A curate comes in from the opposite side holding a censer and positions himself near the platform, to the right, facing the nave. The parish priest appears via a camouflaged door on the right wall of the chancel. He zigzags to the lectern, accompanied by an out-of-tune harmonium. At the same time, two altar boys—ushered in by Turiddu, Teresa's cousin —one carrying a bell, the other one some kind of bowl, station themselves along the right side of the chancel across from the platform. Turiddu looms a hairbreadth behind them. I look at Teresa.

"He's a volunteer," she whispers. "He likes being around

kids. He teaches them catechism, you know ... That kind of stuff."

"Catechism?"

"Yes, why?"

I don't say anything.

The mike on the lectern switches on with a loud screech. The speakers, mounted on the columns throughout the loggia, pop and crackle. A loud buzz follows. Someone must be fiddling with the controls, for the buzzing sound fluctuates; at first, by mistake I imagine, it's turned up so high it causes many of the attendees including the parish priest to cover their ears; within seconds, however, to everyone's great relief, the loud buzz is supplanted by a soft hum. The priest tests the mike with a gentle tap. And after a brief exchange of glances with the curate, he commences the funeral mass by outstretching his arms, signalling the congregation to stand up.

Just then, one of the side doors of the foyer groans open, letting in a wedge of sunlight. The whole congregation turns around—thousands of prying stares levelled at the narthex. It's Marinella, holding hands with the same lady she came into the burial chamber the day before. Clad in a contoured black-purple knee-long dress, Marinella stands there in the central aisle by the last rows of pews. It's but a brief moment, yet charged—judging by the vacuum-sealed atmosphere, as if all the attendees are holding their breaths.

The lady and the little girl, sombrely, start walking down the aisle. I don't know what it is exactly, but there's something different about Marinella; her compliant demeanour

gives off a surprising docility, a far cry from yesterday's way-
ward outbursts and recalcitrance. By the time they reach
the front pews, the widow is there to greet them. She takes
Marinella's hand and walks her to her side. I can hardly see
her now; even so, I find it difficult to take my eyes off her.

The Parish priest resumes mass.

* * *

Between the far too many litanies and the priest's tedious
and somewhat mechanical voice, it's hard to keep one's eyes
open, especially for someone as hungover as I am. Indeed,
during the seemingly endless obsequies, I catch myself dozing off more than once. I'm not the only one, however, given
the many suspiciously stooped mourners. Near the end of
the liturgy, because of the creaking of the aging pews, the
constant rustling of clothes, and the ever-increasing coughing and throat clearings, it is virtually impossible to decipher
anything the mumbling priest utters.

At last, with unexpected vitality and clarity, the priest
pronounces conclusive-sounding words: "*Benediciamo al
Signore ... Rendiamo grazie a Dio.*"

The mass is finally over. An overwhelming wave of
relief sweeps throughout the congregation, and like mushrooms after an autumn rain many of the stooped mourners
suddenly spring up.

"Don't get too excited! He's not done yet," Teresa says
with a mocking smile.

"What do you mean?" My tone must be exuding dis-
tress, for Teresa can barely keep from laughing out loud.

"He's gonna do the final commendation at the cemetery."

"I see."

"Relax. I'm teasing you. We don't have to attend that. You can if you want to, but that's usually reserved for family and close friends."

Aided by the curator, the priest walks off the platform and positions himself in the central aisle, waiting for the pallbearers to gather around the bier. At his signal, a subtle bow that is, the pallbearers, now poised, lift the coffin, slowly descend the altar's steps and—preceded by the priest and the curator, joined by the altar boys and Turiddu—move down the walkway toward the narthex. The chief mourners, this time with Marinella in front alongside her mother, file behind the casket. The procession is halfway through the nave when the main door of the church opens, flooding the loggia with bleached sunlight. Teresa tugs at my arm and, before I can even react, drags me to the central aisle where, together with the other mourners, we follow the procession.

Outside the basilica, we parade through a never-ending human corridor. At the end of it, I spot the hearse, as well as a brass band at the ready beyond it, and two village idiots standing by the back door holding poles with purple banners. One of the two simpletons is short and filthy and with a face reminiscent of a banana: long, concave, and shockingly jaundiced; the other one, the right opposite: tall, husky, dark-skinned, and mouth protruding like that of an ape.

Concomitantly with the placing of the casket into the hearse, the brass band bursts into a jazzy funeral march. But the *attacco* is so sudden and graceless, not to mention utterly discordant, it startles some of the mourners, causing others to cringe. Thankfully, within a couple of minutes, though still rough by any standards, the band players manage to harmonize. A municipal policeman gets off the motorcade parked in front of the band and motions to the hearse's driver to get a move on. I don't see anybody getting into cars or anything of that kind. It looks like we're walking to the cemetery, which, according to Teresa, is right outside the village. It must be close, I reckon. The procession commences.

* * *

Forty-five minutes of painfully slow uphill walk with the sun beating down on our necks and excruciating music: It's a miracle nobody has dropped senseless to the ground. Save for the hearse and the immediate family, we're still at the gate, waiting to get in. Scalloped walls demarcate the cemetery's perimeter, which strikes me as exceptionally large for a village of this size. Its proportion is not the sole peculiar thing about it. From outside the walls on the east side of the gate, four verdigris lighting poles, fifteen to twenty metres in height, like those found in a stadium, tower against the sky. I suppose that explains the larger than usual allotted area for the departed. As we proceed through the threshold, I get visual confirmation. The walled in area is split in the middle by a eucalyptus-treed walkway, skirted on either side by a separation wall. On the left-hand side of the path, there's in fact a football field with just one small concrete bleacher, and on the right side of the path, of course, the cemetery.

By the time we arrive at the opposite end of the walkway, at least half of the mourners, especially the older ones, have already slipped away. The procession comes to a stop in front of another gate; this one leads to the burial ground, clearly visible from where we're standing. I'm not sure what the holdup is, though. "Why are we stopping again?" I whisper to Teresa.

"The coffin is being placed inside the little mortuary for the last salutations," she answers.

"I'm not sure I'm following. I thought you said that the priest was going to recite the last commendation."

"He is. At the burial site."

"Oh," I say, although I'm still not quite clear on the process.

Ten minutes elapse before we make it to the mortuary: a tiny room with no windows, eggshell walls, and a large fridge. Tommasini's casket lies in the centre, on the slab. The funeral attendees circle the coffin in a single file. Most of them kiss their hands and in turn touch the casket as a way of farewell; a handful of others, mostly women, lean over to kiss the casket directly. I don't do either.

Out of the mortuary, I'm amazed to see how rapidly the drove of mourners, who no more than one-and-a-half hours earlier crowded every centimetre of the basilica, has considerably thinned, almost entirely dissipated. I also notice the absence of Tommasini's family along with that of the parish priest, the curator, the altar boys, and apparently Turiddu. I inquire with Teresa.

"They're in the small chapel," she says. "They're waiting for the last salutations to be over."

"Oh, I see."

"What do you say? You wanna head back?"

"Now?"

"Why? Don't tell me you wanna stay for the last commendation? ... No offence, but you looked like you wanted to off yourself during mass! Plus, as I said, it's really for relatives and close friends."

I'm about to concoct some kind of excuse when Ciuzza, the Junoesque proprietress of the Lilliputian bar, calls out Teresa's name from across the cemetery's courtyard. She quickly joins us. "Oh, hello there Mr. ... "

"De Angelis."

"Right. How are you? Good, I hope!" I nod. "Good. Very good." And with an impish grin, she goes on to say: "You're looking dapper in that suit, by the way."

I don't know what to say to that.

"Who did you come with?" Teresa asks.

"Giovannella."

"Where is she?"

"I don't know ... I think I lost her. No matter. You two heading back?"

"I think so," Teresa says. "Are we?" She asks me.

"I think I'll stay a while longer. Why don't you go ahead without me?"

"You sure?"

"Yes, it's no problem. Really. Anyway, it sounds like you two have things to talk about." Teresa shrugs her shoulders. "I'll catch up with you."

"All right. I suppose we'll see you at Tommasini's house." I give her a questioning look. "To express our condolences."

"Yes, of course. Sure, I'll see you there."

I watch them walk away, cross the gate, and disappear into the tree-lined path.

* * *

The mortuary is empty now. In the courtyard, not more than a scattering of mourners linger, waiting, I'm assuming, for the final commendation. Turiddu steps out of the chapel. He sees me and waves at me. I wave back. His exit is immediately followed by that of Alfio accompanied by the other pallbearers and the rest of Tommasini's family, as well as that of the parish priest, the curator, and the altar boys. Without scores of funeral attendees around me, and the complicity of dimmed lighting, I have no chance to evade Alfio.

As he crosses to the morgue, his eyes and mine inevitably lock. He stops and stands there in the middle of the courtyard, dead still, his face granitic. More than a few paces separate us; yet, it's like we're standing but a nose apart from each other. The rest of the pallbearers seem to become aware, quite abruptly, that Alfio is lagging behind. Baffled, judging by their body language, they halt in mid-stride and stare in his direction. Alfio doesn't acknowledge them, his eyes unwaveringly trained on me. All of them—the pallbearers, the remaining mourners, and even Tommasini's family—shift their attention to me. Not until the most uncomfortable, seemingly eternal, moments wear on does the widow with Marinella in tow walk to her brother. They whisper something to one another. Then, as in a moment of sudden realization, the widow starts toward me like a shot.

"Are you De Angelis?" she says, her eyes inflamed. Her whole body shakes.

"Yes," I barely manage to say. She doesn't say anything. She just stares at me, breathing fast and noisily. "Um ... I was going to come talk to you after ... I don't know how to even begin to express how deeply ... *deeply* sorry I am about your husband—"

"Enough!"

"Pardon me?"

Her eyes tear up. Her shaking intensifies. "Don't you dare talk to me!" she says. Though taken aback, and despite her warning, I motion to say something, but she cuts me right off. "You ... *You* should've died! Not my Peppe! ... You!"

I'm stunned.

The words spurt out of her mouth with such violence, they hit me with the unexpectedness and tactile potency of a backhand. I want to leave at once, but I feel paralyzed.

Likely prompted by the widow's outburst, Alfio runs to us. "Calm down," he says, gesturing to a lady across the courtyard to come over. "Look at me." She's still shaking. "You've got to calm down ... Take a deep breath ... Good ... That's it ... That's it." The lady arrives, takes the widow by the arm, and walks her back to the chapel. "What did I say to you, yesterday?"

"I'm sorry, I didn't mean to—"

"What did I tell you?"

"I'm—"

"*What did I tell you?*"

I turn around and rush out of the cemetery. As I start off down the walkway, I hear someone call my name. I look about me. It's Calò, leaning on a eucalyptus by the gate, on the path's side. He straightens up and ambles down the lane. We meet halfway. He's wearing his Sunday best. I almost didn't recognize him.

"How are you?" he says, lighting up a cigarette.

"How am I? ... Really? ... No offence, but I'm in no mood for formalities. Put it in second gear."

"I see ... Cards-on-the-table time, huh?"

"What does that even mean?"

"I get it. You're upset right now. So, I'm gonna gloss over your hostile tone. All right? ... You know ... I heard what Tommasini's wife said to you before. That's gotta be rough—"

"Out with it. What is it? Another threat?"

"Threat? What threat? Nobody is threatening anybody. You know ... You might wanna choose your words more carefully, my dear De Angelis. Some people might get offended."

"Look, the deal's off. We're not buying that goddam property. So why on earth are you still following me?"

"Following?"

"Was that you in the white car the other day?"

"Careful, you're starting to sound a little paranoid!"

"Am I?"

"I'm not following anybody. I'm here to mourn a friend. I'm not sure I can say the same about you."

"What's that supposed to mean?"

"I don't know ... I don't know ... Be well, Mr. De Angelis."

Chapter Eighteen

"**W**ait up! ... De Angelis ... Mr. De Angelis!" It's Turiddu, running toward me. "Hold on a minute. Wait for me!"

"What's the matter?" I ask.

Turiddu gestures me to wait a second. "Damn you walk fast!" he says, as he catches his breath.

"What is it?"

"Oh no, nothing."

"What do you mean *nothing*? ... You ran all this way for nothing?"

"I wanted to walk with you. You don't mind, do you?"

"I guess ... But what about the last commendation? Is that over already?"

"No. Not yet ... Truth is, I couldn't take another one of the priest's soporific litanies. Half the people in that church were comatose. Am I wrong? Honestly?" I shake my head. "Don't get me wrong. He's a very nice man, very smart.

It's just … I don't know … Anyway, everybody is waiting for him to retire."

"I had the impression you were in charge of the altar boys," I say, as we start off to the village.

"Who? Me? … No, I help out a little … You know?"

"Perhaps, I misunderstood."

"How so?"

"Your cousin mentioned something about you teaching catechism, I think she said, to these boys … Anyway, it doesn't matter. Forget it."

"Anything to keep away from my mother, my dear De Angelis. Anything." For some reason, I don't believe a single word he says. I drop it anyhow. "So … That was a real heart-grabber before, huh? … What happened between you and the widow? … Maybe, you don't wanna talk about it."

"She's in pain."

"What's that?"

"She's in *pain* I said!"

"Even still, that was outta line. I mean … that was a cruel thing to say, wasn't it? I don't know how I would react, frankly. If someone said something like that to me—"

"Look, she's grieving. I'm sure she didn't mean it."

"Wow, I gotta say … You're taking this extremely well—"

"Do you mind if we talk about something else?"

"Of course. My apologies. It didn't realize I was upsetting you."

"It's all right."

"We can talk about any topic you like."

"Good."

Aside from a couple of false starts, neither one of us speaks a single word. In fact, all the way down to the village, we remain completely quiet. It's only once we reach the main square that Turiddu breaks the silence. "Well, that's my stop." I give him a look. "I have some cleanup to do in the church."

"Oh."

"All right." Turiddu makes as if to leave but stops right away. "Teresa tells me you're sticking around a while longer, is that right?" I nod. "I'll see you around, then."

I watch him trot to the basilica and, about to step inside it, wave at me one more time. I reciprocate. It occurs to me, all of a sudden, that Teresa and Ciuzza are probably waiting for me at Tommasini's house. I have to get there before the last commendation is over. By the time I arrive, there's already a block-long queue of people waiting to express their condolences to the widow. Teresa and Ciuzza must've been the first ones to get here, for they are standing at the head of the line, by the door, eagerly waving at me. I walk to them. They both welcome me with unwarranted broad smiles.

"We thought you were gonna bail on us," Teresa says. "Come, come. You can stand right here."

"I'm afraid I can't stay."

"How come?"

I get closer to Teresa and Ciuzza and take my voice down to a whisper, too many eyes and ears within range. "I have to leave before Tommasini's brother-in-law gets here."

"Why?" Ciuzza asks.

"I'm not welcome here. The widow is very upset by my presence."

"But why?" Teresa asks.

"I'm not sure why. I know it doesn't make much sense; however, I do feel that I have to respect their wishes. I don't want to be the cause of unnecessary pain. Anyway, I just wanted to let you know. I didn't want you to wait for me here needlessly."

"Sure, of course. Thanks for telling us."

"All right."

"You coming for dinner?"

"If you want me to, I will." She nods. "I'll be there."

* * *

On my way back to the lodging, I decide to take a detour to the flower shop to buy a bouquet or something for Teresa. As I'm crossing the main square in the direction of the burial services shop, I spot Turiddu squeeze himself out of the boarded-up entrance of the unfinished hideous building. The bottom right corner of the corrugated metal sheet covering the door is detached. For a moment, Turiddu stands there, looking up and down the street, and then sidles back to the church. I don't think he saw me. Bested by my curiosity, I approach the angular construction. I scan the surroundings to make sure no one is watching. No indiscreet eyes as far as I can see. I lift the metal sheet and carefully slide into the building, trying not to rip my suit. It's dark, but, as my eyes adjust, the sunlight seeping in through the cracks of the boarded-up windows is enough to make out the inside.

As expected, the construction is in complete disarray. Most of the abandoned materials and tools have been either destroyed or partially looted. In almost every room of the ground floor, the walls are daubed with graffiti, for the most part pornographic. The X-rated motif ramps up on the upper floors, at the expense, it seems to me, of detailing and drawing skills, and the higher I go the cruder the graffiti become. So much so that by the time I set foot on the top floor the drawings are nothing but childish scribbles, if that.

One room appears brighter than the others. I enter it. There's a skylight; it's a small one, but large enough to flood the room with sunlight. I'm not sure why but this room gives off a different vibe. Like the other ones, ransacked materials and bits and pieces of airbricks are scattered around; however, four heavy stacks of still intact bags of cement in the middle of room strike me as peculiar. It has something to do not only with the fact they are in pristine condition but also with the way they are positioned. They seem to have been parallel to each other at one point, forming a square. But, based on the markings on the floor, someone has taken the trouble to fan them out slightly, thus creating an isosceles trapezoid. This is definitely not the work of some kid horsing around. They are far too heavy. I suppose Turiddu would've been able to move these, even if not easily. But why would he do such a thing? To what purpose?

I take another look at the space. In one of the corners, someone has gathered a short pile of airbricks. By the way they're stacked up to the wall, it's obvious there's something hidden behind them. No one but a kid would think this is a safe way to hide something. Sure enough, as I reach over, I find a bunch of pornographic magazines bundled up and held together with rubber bands—girl on girl action, anal pleasure, double penetration, interracial, and even animals. This room must be where kids come to masturbate. I slide the magazines back into their hiding place. Still, this doesn't explain the bags of cement being moved. I don't know why it bothers me so much.

I'm about to leave the room, but an electrical receptacle on the wall—mounted at about a couple of palms from the floor and at exactly the mid-point of the wall—grabs my attention. Unless I'm mistaken, it seems to be the only electrical receptacle installed on any of the walls. It has two outlets; the top one is a little sunk in. At closer inspection, it becomes clear that this receptacle doesn't even belong on the wall. It doesn't quite fit into the metal outlet box. By the looks of it, I'd say someone jammed it in. I poke at the recessed one. As soon as I touch it, the outlet falls inside the box, leaving a black hole in its stead. I bend over to look through it. I can see the adjacent room from it. Apparently, the person who put the receptacle on the wall has also gone through the trouble to cut out the back of the metal outlet box.

I get up and go to the adjoining room. There's no access to it; a wall of poorly laid airbricks serves as barricade. Aside from a slim gap between the lintel and the partition, the entrance to the room is entirely closed off. The sloppy work suggests the hand of an amateur as opposed to that of a professional stonemason. There has got to be another way to access that room. It occurs to me it must be through the balcony. I can't see any other way to get to it. As it happens, one of the boarded-up openings giving onto the street is loose enough to get through. It does in fact lead to a balcony with no rails. At the far end of it, I can see a blockaded window. On one side of it, the boards sealing it off are loose. I lift them up and squeeze myself through it.

Without a doubt, this is the room. I leave the boards a tad ajar to let some light in. Footprints all over the floor, a plastic crate with a cushion on it, and some kind of drop cloth on the floor corroborate my suspicions. The dust-sheet is stretched out right under a hole on the wall, which is at about two palms from the floor. I lie down on the cloth. The opening is exactly where the metal box and receptacle are on the other side of the wall. From this vantage point, I can see a great deal of the adjacent room, especially the stacks of cement. It dawns on me that the bags have been purposefully fanned out so as to have an unobstructed view of whoever sits on them.

* * *

I lift the corrugated metal sheet, slide out of the building, and set foot onto the curb. The shift from gloomy to bright light blinds me at first, to the point that I have to shield my eyes. It doesn't take too long for my vision to normalize. Quickly, I survey the street to make sure nobody saw me. That's when I clap eyes on Turiddu. He's leaning on the wall at the corner where the street opens out on to the piazza. He's peering my way. We stare at each other for a time, but neither one of us makes a move. No more than a minute or two go by, however, before Turiddu walks off around the corner.

* * *

At the flower shop, I find Tano behind the desk. I didn't figure he'd be there. For whatever reason, I thought he was at the funeral. He too seems quite surprised, if not perturbed, to see me entering his establishment. There's no one else in the store but us.

"Mr. De Angelis ... Did you forget something? ... I didn't find anything lying around. Not that I looked really. But ... "

"No, that's not it. I didn't forget anything."

"Oh ... So, to what do I owe this pleasure?"

"I'm here to get some flowers—"

"For Tommasini? I already made the garland with what's his name on it? ... Montanari, is it?"

"No, no, this is something else ... It's for my landlady. Teresa Giuffrè? You know her?" he nods. "Well ... Um ... I'm looking for a gift for her, as a thank you, if you will."

"Oh, I see ... Let's have a look." He steps out from behind the desk and walks to the flower display. "I think I know what Mrs. Giuffrè likes."

"Do you?"

"I'm pretty sure she'll be pleased with this one." Tano is holding the tackiest and the most colourful of the terracotta flowerpots—it has trinkets and tulle as ornaments.

"You think so?"

"Positive ... So, what do you say? ... Should I wrap it up?"

"Please."

* * *

"In here," Teresa yells. And as I enter the kitchen: "You made it." She's watching another one of those trashy telenovelas. "What's that?"

"This? It's for you."

"For me? ... Why, thank you! ... I don't know what to say."

"It's nothing really. Here ... " The way she's staring at the wrapping, I'd say she hasn't received a gift in years. She's so overwhelmed by my gesture that she appears unsure where to even begin taking the wrapping apart. Eventually, I see her reaching for a pair of scissors. "Let me give you a hand with that. See this? All you have to do is pull it. That's it."

"Don't I feel silly!" she says, a touch flushed. "Thank you! This is truly beautiful."

"You like it?"

"Very much. Thank you." Her voice breaks slightly, her face steeped in pure joy.

"I'm glad you're pleased with it ... Um ... Listen, do I have time to get changed? Maybe even take a shower?"

"Yes, of course. It's still very early. You even have time to lie down a while if you want to rest your leg. How is it, by the way?"

"It's fine, better actually."

"Good. That's good."

"All right." I move to the door. "Oh, I almost forgot ... "

"What is it?"

"I fell before—"

"God! Where? Are you hurt?"

"No, no, nothing like that. I'm totally fine ... It's the suit ... I'm afraid I got some dirt on it. It's not ripped or anything—"

"Oh, don't worry about that. I'll take it to the cleaners."

"I'd like to pay for that though. Please?"

"Would you stop? Go ahead. Go freshen up."

* * *

A violent rap at the door yanks me out of a nightmare. I half sit up, feeling a shade nauseated. Another even more forceful knocking follows.

"Mr. De Angelis!" It's Teresa. "Mr. De Angelis, you have a phone call!" I go to the door and crack it open. "Oh, you're up … Good."

"Sorry, I fell asleep. What time is it?"

"It's almost eight—"

"Eight! It feels like I just went down five minutes ago … Next thing I know it's eight o'clock and you're taking the door down."

"Oh, I'm sorry. Was that too loud?"

"No matter. You said I have a phone call?"

"Yes. You can probably guess who."

"Montanari?"

"You guessed it!"

"I'll be right down. Let me throw some water on my face."

* * *

"Hello?"

"De Angelis?"

"Yes."

"Finally! You're a hard man to reach, you know that?"

"Sorry—"

"So … Where do we stand? You were supposed to keep me informed. Remember?"

"I know."

"Do you?" I slowly lower myself on to the stool by the hall-tree stand. "All right, why don't you give me an update?"

"Okay ... Well ... Tommasini was buried today."

"I see ... How were the flowers?"

"The flowers? Oh, yes, of course. They were great. The florist did a really good job with it."

"Excellent, excellent ... What else?"

"Right ... As I already mentioned, we'll resume talks now."

"When?"

"Tomorrow or the day after, I think."

"'*Tomorrow*,' '*The day after*,' ... What is this?"

"What do you mean?"

"Is it tomorrow or the day after? Which one is it?"

Montanari's aggressive obstinacy catches me a bit off-guard. "It's not set yet," I manage to say, somewhat hesitantly. "They're going to let me know."

"When? It's eight o'clock already!"

"Yes, I'm aware of that. They should be calling me here any time now."

"Mm ... I see ... All right, I'll let you go for now. However — and I cannot stress this strongly enough — set up a meet as soon as possible, no more postponing. You've been down there for what? Five days now?"

"Yes."

"Exactly!"

"It's not my fault if things happened the way they did," I say, without a moment's thought.

"I'm not saying that ... Look, I sympathize with the widow and everybody. It is a small town after all, and most likely they all know each other. I can appreciate that ... but it's time to expedite things now ... Agreed?"

"Agreed."

"Good. I want a full report in two days. Don't make me call *you*."

As I hang up the phone, I hear rustling of clothes behind me. I swivel back.

"Oh, it's you."

"I didn't wanna interrupt," Teresa says. Her voice and body language betray guilt. "Anyway, dinner is almost ready." She makes a start.

"How long have you been standing there?"

She stops. "What's that?"

"How long were you there for?"

"Not long. Why?"

The promptness of her answer implies otherwise.

"Nothing," I tell her, getting up. "Shall we?" Entering the kitchen, I notice four settings on the table. "Who else is coming?"

"Oh, didn't I tell you?" I shake my head. "My cousin and my aunt. I hope you don't mind." I shake my head again. "He actually kind of invited himself."

"How do you mean?"

"Well ... he came by and asked if *you* were coming for dinner ... "

"Did he?"

She nods.

"I said yes and ... you know ... one thing led to another and ... here we are." The doorbell rings. "Speaking of the devil! ... Excuse me."

Teresa beetles off to the door. I remain in the middle of the kitchen. Five minutes go by and still no sign of them. Not knowing what to do with myself and overcome by a puerile urge to see what's going on, I move toward the door, and that's when I hear them coming. The squeal of some kind wheelchair precedes them.

"Mr. De Angelis! Long time no see!" Turiddu says, wheeling his mother in. I force a smile. "Mom, this is Mr. De Angelis, Teresa's lodger."

"How do you do?" I walk to her and offer to shake her hand. She doesn't reciprocate. There's something utterly repulsive about her: her eyes, thyroidal; her mouth, frozen in perpetual contempt; her large figure, bubbled like an over-leavened bread.

"What are you? You from the North or something?" She asks with her froggy voice.

"Yes. Milan."

"Milan? ... *Gesù*, Giuseppe, *e* Maria! You got fog up there, don't you?"

"Sometimes."

"Snow too, no?"

"Yes, snow too."

"Oh my God, look at you! You're white as a sheet! You look like a ghost!"

"All right, mom. That's enough." Turiddu helps his mother out of the wheelchair and hands her a cane, which she uses to walk to the table. Turiddu tries to accompany her, but she shrugs him off. "All right. You good, mom?"

"Yes, yes, yes ... Leave me be!"

A fit of bile warps Turiddu's face. We all take a seat at the dining table. Not by choice, I find myself sitting across from that vile, slatternly old bag. The mere thought of having to look at her brings on a third-degree nausea. As she shifts in her chair, fetid whiffs of stale sweat smell up the place. I regurgitate in my mouth. I'm not sure how I'm going to get through dinner like this.

"You all right?" Teresa asks.

"Yes ... I'm still a little hungover. That's all."

"You didn't eat today, did you?" I shake my head. "Poor thing, you must be starving!" Teresa jumps to her feet and walks to the counter. "You'll feel better as soon as you put something in your stomach. Trust me." Turiddu joins her to lend a hand plating. The ghastly old bat doesn't take her bugged out eyes off me.

"There you are," Teresa says, lowering a plate with some kind of baked ring-shaped pasta on it. "That's *anelletti*. Have you ever had it?"

"No."

"It has *ragù*, and in the middle it's got melted *provolone*."

"Teresa, where's the wine?" Turiddu asks.

"The refrigerator."

He walks to the fridge, takes out a bottle of wine, and opens it at the table. And after giving everybody, including his mother, a generous pour, he raises his glass. "*Cin Cin.*"

Teresa and I follow his lead. Turiddu's mother is already gnawing away at her food like a cow chewing the cud.

"So," Turiddu says, sitting down, "I heard you got yourself into some trouble." I throw him a look. He points at the bruises on my face. "Teresa tells me you don't remember how it happened, is that right?"

I look at Teresa. She's a touch flushed. I can tell, though, she wasn't expecting Turiddu would bring this up. "Yes. That's right."

"Wow. I can't imagine how that's even possible."

"Turiddu!" Teresa says.

"What? ... I'm just wondering. That's all. Never happened to me." Turiddu takes a big spoonful of pasta and shoves it into his mouth. "Mmm ... Teresa, this is delicious! Isn't it, De Angelis?"

"Yes, it is. It's really good."

"I'll tell you, though," Turiddu says, his mouth still full, "I can't get it out of my mind ... "

"What are you talking about?" Teresa asks.

"Nothing."

"No, what?"

"Nothing, something Mrs. Tommasini said today, that's all."

"What? What'd she say to you?"

"No, not to me."

"Who, then?" Turiddu points at me with a tilt of his head. "You? ... What'd she say to you?"

I give a sidelong look at Turiddu. "It's not important," I say, trying to diffuse the moment.

"She said that *him* should've died, not Peppe."

"Turiddu! ... Why would you say something like that?"

"I didn't. *She* did."

"Is that true?" I nod. "That's a horrible thing to say. I cannot believe she actually said that to you."

"It's quite all right. She's in pain. I'm pretty sure she didn't mean it."

"Even so—"

"You know ... " Turiddu says. "I can't, for the life of

me, wrap my head around this ... How's it possible that ... someone ... hits you in the face, because that's what it looks like, and you don't even remember it!"

"Leave him alone," Teresa shouts. Then to me: "Sorry. He's got no manners. Shit-bag that he is, he doesn't know when to stop."

"It's all right—"

"Why do you always make me out to be some kinda country cousin?" Turiddu says.

"I think you can answer your own question, Inspector Clouseau!"

"What did you call me—"

"*Basta*!" the old bag says. "*Signuruzzu beddu*! ... *Tutti dui scimuniti siti*! ... *Nun cuntati nenti, comu u dui i mazzi quannu a briscola e coppi*! ... *Nun vogghiu sentiri natra parola*! *Mancu na musca vogghiu sentiri vulari*!"

For the rest of the dinner not a single word is uttered at the table. Only the cadenced gnawing of food and clinking of silver disrupts the otherwise morose silence.

* * *

"De Angelis, let's go for a smoke," Turiddu says. I hesitate. "Come on! Keep me company."

"You ... Behave yourself!" Teresa says.

"Why are you getting all bent out of shape? Just going for a smoke, that's all."

"I'll make some coffee."

Apart from a couple of elders sitting on their front stoops, there's no one outside.

"Lovely night, huh," Turiddu says, lighting a cigarette.

I don't comment on it. "Say ... What were you doing inside that construction today? ... If you don't mind my asking, of course!"

"I could ask you the same question."

Turiddu takes a big drag on his cigarette. His eyes tighten and, while exhaling, looks away. His head slightly cocks downward. He maintains that posture for a moment or two. And after inhaling another big puff of smoke, he turns to me again. "I saw you talking to Calò today." I shrug my shoulders. "Do you know him?"

"Why?"

"I'm curious. Is he involved in this deal ... thing you got going?"

"No ... Not that this is any of your business, but he was asking about my leg."

"Your leg?"

"He's the one who rescued me from the dogs."

"Calò?"

"Yes, Calò."

He takes one final drag on his cigarette, throws the butt on the curb, and steps on it. "Do you know who he is?"

"Who, Calò? I told you—"

"No. I mean ... Do you know who he represents?"

"I'm afraid I'm not following."

"You don't, huh? ... Why don't you wanna tell us what happened to your face?"

"I told you—"

"Yes, yes, you said. You don't remember ... You know, you can fool Teresa, but not me."

"What's that supposed to mean?"

Turiddu walks back into the house.

* * *

Teresa's cousin and his mother leave not too long after drinking their coffee. Teresa and I—me looking at her sideways, she staring off into the distance, her brow a touch furrowed—sit there a while without speaking, partly, I'm assuming, for digestive reasons and, perhaps, partly because of the most welcome quietude. I soon realize, however, there's more to Teresa's silence than digestive issues and a yearning for peacefulness. Something's brewing in her head. I'm not sure what, though. All I'm certain of is that she lied about eavesdropping on me while I was on the phone with Montanari. I wonder how much of it she actually caught or understood even. But I can tell this is bothering her.

As though suddenly able to read my thoughts, she turns to me. We lock eyes. She can barely hold my gaze. She looks away for a moment and back to me again with a manufactured smile. She then hoists herself up and walks to the sink where a mountain of grease-stained dishes awaits. I offer to help. She refuses. I insist, but she won't have it.

"You should rest," she says. "You must feel exhausted, no?"

"I am a bit ragged … I'm not going to lie to you. Your cousin has worn me to a frazzle."

"I know exactly how you feel. Except, you don't have to live with it. Well, not for much longer, anyhow."

"Right."

"I'm sorry. Sometimes I open my mouth without thinking. I didn't mean to imply that you have to leave. *Per carità*! … You can stay as long as you like at no charge. I'm serious."

"Thank you. It's much appreciated." I start off to my room. "Um … Look … "

"What is it?"

"Before … When I was talking to Montanari—"

"I told you—" I signal her to let me finish.

"I'm not sure of what you heard, or what you thought you heard rather … It's not what it looks like … Yes, I haven't told him yet that the deal's off. Truth is, I thought that while I was still here waiting for the funeral I should at least try to fix it."

"Did you?"

I shake my head. "Now I'm basically looking for a way to ease the news to him."

"I see."

"I must seem pretty silly to you right now."

"Not at all. Quite the contrary."

"All right. I'm off to bed."

"I meant it before. You can stay as long as you like."

"Goodnight."

"Night."

❧ Chapter Nineteen

It's still dark in the room. I don't see any light of sunup spilling in yet. I try to reach for the alarm clock on the bed-side table, but somehow I feel constrained. Perhaps, I'm dreaming. It's the strangest thing, though. Everything is so vivid—too vivid to be merely a concoction of my brain. I briefly close my eyes. Once more, I reach for the alarm clock. This time my body responds.

It's five past three, according to the clock's fluores-cent-green hands. I let go of the clock and lie back down on the bed. That little sleep I had must've been restless, for I find the sheets absurdly wound tight around my body. The room is so musty, I can hardly breathe. The little fan on the dresser is practically useless. My mouth is complete-ly dry. Still a bit hazy, I sit up and stuff a pillow behind my back. Suddenly, as if it weren't there a second ago, I become acutely conscious of a burning sensation crawling up my oesophagus.

I untangle myself from the sheets and stand up in an attempt to ease the heartburn but also on account of the sheets being soaked through with sweat. I walk to the window and pull the mosquito net away from the shutter. All the slats on the two-panelled jalousie are already angled open, so I unfasten both sides of the shutter and push them apart to allow more fresh air in. It's no use. There's no wind to speak of. I lean on the sill and stick my head out the window. A low, dense mass of clouds has curtained the sky from corner to corner, pushing down on the village like an airtight lid.

Besides the occasional wailing and yowling of cats and dogs and the more isolated cry of some other obscure creature of the night, the town is dead still. It occurs to me that I should, perhaps, crack the door open as well, on the off chance it might create some kind of airflow. It takes a little while, but it seems to work; and though it isn't much, it does get some breeze going. I carefully lift the one chair in the room, trying to avoid making any noise, and place it exactly where the draft is at its strongest. I strip naked and sit there to dry off. Within a minute, maybe less, I can feel my eyelids, still leaden with sleep, or the lack of it rather, slowly drawing shut. Just as I'm dozing off, the grating sound of a steel shutter causes me to sit bolt upright. It must be the baker or something.

I sink back into the chair, reflexively staring off somewhere outside the window. It doesn't take long, however, for the gaze to turn inward. I don't even know if my eyes are still open. Fragments of images flash before my eyes. Nothing concrete. Nothing I can grasp, same as the debris of dreams, or nightmares rather, I can't either remember or fathom. I try to stop it, but it only worsens. The fragmentary images give way to an infectious cataract of malformed thoughts, pressing down on my brow like a sinusitis.

* * *

A gentle knock at the door wakes me up, but I'm still far too dazed to move or make a sound.

"Mr. De Angelis?" Teresa calls out. "You up? Can I come in?" Before I can answer, she's already pushing the door open. "Hello? ... Where are yo—Oh, there you are. What are you doing on the fl—*O Gesù miu*!" Teresa freezes a few paces from the door. Her hands shield her mouth, her face glowing red. "I'm so sorry," she says, stammering. "I didn't mean to ... The door was open ... I ... I'm sorry ... "

She turns on her heels and rushes out, banging the door behind her. I can hear her going down the stairs so fast I'm afraid she's going to hurt herself. At first, I'm baffled by her behaviour; then, I realize I'm lying on the tiled floor completely naked. No wonder she ran out of here. I throw some clothes on as fast as I can and make for the stairs. As I cross the landing, the front door slams shut. I suppose she's too embarrassed to talk right now.

I swing back to my room, get undressed again, and hop in the shower. There must be some kind of water shortage, for the shower shuts off short of rinsing my hair. Not sure how to proceed I stand there in the shower waiting for God knows what. Finally it dawns on me that I should probably take a look at the faucets on the ground floor; there could be some residual water in the pipes. I swiftly wind a towel around my waist and head downstairs. It turns out

I'm right. I manage to retrieve almost a bucket-full of water from the kitchen sink.

Back in my room, I quickly rinse my hair, dry off, change the bandages on my bum leg, slip into some fresh clothes, and head back down. In the rashness of the moment, I didn't realize that Teresa had prepared some breakfast for me. It's neatly laid out on the table; there's even some coffee left in the *caffettiera*, still warm. I pour myself a demitasse, have a few bites of a ricotta *cornetto*, which doesn't seem to go down well, and put away the rest of the food. I don't want it to spoil. On my way out, I spot a little note taped on the outside of the door:

> *Mr. De Angelis, I'm really sorry about what*
> *happened. I didn't mean to walk in on you like*
> *that. The door was open. Otherwise, I would*
> *never have entered your room without permission.*
> *I know I did once (to clean and put some clothes*
> *in the closet), but at least I knew you weren't*
> *there. Not that I make it a habit to go in your*
> *room when you're not there. You know what I*
> *mean. Anyway, I'm really sorry about that.*
> *You've probably figured out by the time you read*
> *this that there's no running water in the house.*
> *Unfortunately, the cisterns up on the terrace are*
> *empty. But don't worry, I'll have a truck-full of*
> *water delivered hopefully later this afternoon. I*
> *apologize for the inconvenience. Also, I won't be*
> *home for lunch, so I'm afraid you have to fend for*
> *yourself today.*

The note was written in such a hurry that the hand-writing is barely legible.

* * *

As I'm walking down to the main square to grab another coffee, I hear a car horn, blasting from a good distance behind me, immediately followed by a voice calling my name. I turn to it. It's the *Brigadiere*'s. He's at the wheel of the *Carabinieri*'s armoured jeep, signalling me to wait. His boss is sitting next to him. The street I'm on is a one-way, so the jeep has to go around to meet me.

"Mr. De Angelis," the *Maresciallo* calls out. I walk up to him. "Good morning."

"Morning."

"We were looking for you."

"Why?"

"Where are you headed?"

"I beg your pardon?"

"Hop in. We'll give you a lift to wherever … "

"I was going down to the piazza for a cup of coffee."

"Excellent! We were gonna do just that, weren't we?"

"Precisely," the *Brigadiere* says.

"It'll be my pleasure to buy you one."

"You don't need to bother. Besides, I enjoy walking—"

"Get in the car!"

"Excuse me!"

"You heard him!" the *Brigadiere* shouts. His puffed cheeks balloon up even more when he's angry. For a second, I consider my answer. Obviously, it's a second too long, for the *Brigadiere* flounces out of the jeep, comes around, and walks right up to my face, stopping barely a palm away from me, snorting like a bull. "Get in the damn car! Right now!"

I abstain from dragging this any longer and climb into the back seat.

"Now, was that so hard?" the *Maresciallo* says, glancing at me from the rear-view mirror.

"Where to?" the *Brigadiere* asks, addressing the *Maresciallo*. "*Don Paolino*'s?"

"No. Last time the coffee was burnt."

"*Egisto*'s then?"

The *Maresciallo* nods.

At the piazza, the *Brigadiere* double-parks the vehicle right in front of a bar called *Da Egisto*. Except for the time I was looking for a pay phone, I haven't really been into this establishment. Of the bars in the square, this is among the older ones. It seems to me it attracts exclusively die-hard fans: stooped octogenarians wearing wool suits in forty-degree weather. They are all sitting on patio chairs outside the bar, on either side of the entrance, leaning on their canes. There are also a couple of cast-iron round tables outside, both occupied.

"All right, Mr. De Angelis. Here we are." The *Maresciallo* lowers himself out of the jeep, and so do I. The *Brigadiere* lingers behind.

As we step closer to the bar, everybody stops talking. A series of reverential gestures follows: bowing of heads, mostly with a submissive tilt, instantly succeeded by doffing of caps for some, and by emphatic hand sweeps for some others. Three gentlemen sitting at one of the two tables rise to leave, clearing the spot for the *Maresciallo* and me. A youth comes out of the bar with a rag and wipes the table with it. "*Prego*," he says, pointing at the chairs with great deference. The *Maresciallo* and I take a seat opposite each other.

"At your service, *Signor Maresciallo*. How can I have the pleasure to assist you on a fine morning such as this?" the youth says, looking positively too young to be working, let alone in a bar. The youngster's feudal diction flows out with such ease it's hard to believe he isn't more than a teenager. You can't simply pick up this kind of verbiage. It has the hallmarks of a long-standing tradition being passed on from generation to generation.

"Mr. De Angelis, this able young man here is Giacomino."

"How do you do, Mr. De Angelis?"

"How do you do?"

"I hope you're having a glorious morning so far."

"I'll have an iced tea with *granita*," the *Maresciallo* says.

"Lemon? ... Almond?" Giacomino asks. The *Maresciallo* mulls it over. "At the risk of sounding perhaps a touch presumptuous may I recommend almond this morning."

The *Maresciallo* looks at Giacomino with intrigue. "Almond you say, huh?" Giacomino gives him a slanted nod, along with a collusive smile. "What do you think, Mr. De Angelis?" I don't know why he's asking me. I shrug my shoulders. "Almond it is, then."

"With or without brioche?"

"Oh, you little devil! I probably shouldn't, but ... What the hell! With, please."

"And for the gentleman over here?"

"Espresso. *Lungo*, please."

"With immense pleasure." Giacomino dashes into the bar.

"He's something, isn't he?" the *Maresciallo* says.

"You didn't bring me here to talk about Giacomino's fine qualities, did you?"

He signals me to wait. Giacomino reappears from inside the bar, carrying our order on a deep round tray.

"There you are, gentlemen. Tea with *granita* and brioche for the *Maresciallo*, and coffee, *lungo* as per request, for Mr. De Angelis."

"Thank you, Giacomino," the *Maresciallo* says. I thank him as well.

"Well, if you need anything else, please don't hesitate to ask."

"Mr. De Angelis and I need to have a little chat—"

"Say no more." At once, Giacomino makes himself scarce.

The *Maresciallo* halves the brioche and dips one half in the tea-*granita* mixture. "Mmm ... Now, that's how you start a hot morning like this. Delicious! You should try it."

"I'm not hungry, thank you."

By the time I finish my espresso, the *Maresciallo* wolfs down the rest of the brioche and two-thirds of the *granita*. It's astonishing he didn't get a brain freeze.

"So ... Brass tacks ... Why are you still here?"

"I beg your pardon!"

"Please, don't insult my intelligence, Mr. De Angelis."

"I'm not trying to insult anyone's intelligence here. Maybe, you've overestimated mine."

"May*be* ... All right, allow me to ... shall we say? ... break it down for you. Your business transaction or whatever you wanna call it went belly up, am I right? ... After all, you said so yourself in my office, correct?" I nod. "Oh, good. So we understand each other. We're on the same page, shall we say?" I'm starting to get irritated by his tone and his niggling phrase-tag. "Now ... Tommasini's funeral, *bonanima*, was yesterday. Beautiful send off, by the way—"

"Is there a question in there?"

"You got no business here. You've paid your respects, shall we say? And yet here you are ... still in town."

"I'm not an expert of the law, but I seriously doubt this classifies as a crime."

"If I were you, Mr. De Angelis, I wouldn't take that tone with me."

"What tone?"

"Boy! That Montanari sure sounds like a piece of work, doesn't he?"

"Come again?"

"Oh, didn't I tell you?"

"Tell me what?"

"I paid him a call this morning, with the excuse of double-checking some facts. Of course, he didn't know that the case, as in regard to Tommasini, is already closed, but then again he didn't seem to know a lot of things. One in particular struck me as ... quite odd, shall we say? ... Oh, I'm sure there's a perfectly good explanation for it. I just can't wait to hear it." I keep quiet and let him do the talking. "For instance, could you, if you please, explain to me why I had the impression that Montanari, *your boss*, still thinks that you're negotiating the deal with the Colantonio brothers? ... As we speak! ... It's the damnedest thing!"

"Why? What did he say?"

"Let's not split hairs, Mr. De Angelis. It's not so much what he said, but what he didn't say."

"Perhaps, you—"

"Let's cut the crap, shall we? Out with it!"

"Not that this is any of your business ... Truth is, I haven't had the heart to tell him yet ... I was actually planning on telling him tomorrow."

"Why tomorrow? Why not today? What's so special about tomorrow?"

"He thinks I have a meeting with the brothers. I'm supposed to report to him tomorrow."

"I see ... "

"You see?"

"So, Mr. De Angelis, is that it? ... That's all?"

"That's it ... And as I said, this is none of your business. I don't have to justify myself to you—"

"Let's get this straight. *I* tell *you* what *is* and what *isn't* my business!" I don't say anything. "What happened to your face? Don't answer it. It's one of them ... whatchamacallit? ... rhetorical questions. I know exactly how it went down ... And what about Tommasini's widow? That poor woman! As if she hasn't suffered enough already. Or his brother-in-law, Alfio?"

"What about them?"

"I think it's fair to say, Mr. De Angelis, that you've ... overstayed your welcome, shall we say? ... I suggest, in the strongest possible terms, you leave Figallia as soon as you can. Tomorrow seems to be a good day to wrap things up, don't you think?"

"And if I don't?"

"You don't wanna see my darker side, Mr. De Angelis … Giacomino!"

"At your service, *Maresciallo*."

"Put it on my tab, unless Mr. De Angelis here desires something else … "

"I'm fine." Giacomino takes his leave.

"All right," the *Maresciallo* says, getting up. "Don't take this the wrong way, but I sincerely hope I won't see your face again."

He walks to the jeep, gets into the passengers' seat, and rolls down the window. He throws me one more brief look then turns to the *Brigadiere* and with his left hand motions him to take off.

The people sitting at the other table rise to leave as well. Promptly, Giacomino shows up carrying the rag, as though a concealed weapon, in his right hand. He wipes the table with calibrated strokes, folding the rag only once. He catches me scrutinizing him. "Is there something else I can do for you, Mr. De Angelis?"

"What?"

"I said if I could be of service to you." He steps closer to me.

"Oh … "

"I hope you don't mind my saying so, but … Are you all right?"

"I'm fine, thank you."

"Very well, enjoy your day, Mr. De Angelis."

"You know … On second thought, I'll have another coffee."

"Wonderful! I'll fetch that for you straightaway!" Giacomino says, scurrying over to the bar.

"Not so fast." I wave him to come back. "Actually, could you make that a double espresso *corretto* in a big cup?"

"Why, yes, of course. Grappa? ... Sambuca?"

"Grappa, please."

"I shall return shortly."

By the time Giacomino runs back into the bar, I catch a glimpse of Turiddu walking briskly towards the church. I don't think he saw me.

"There you are, Mr. De Angelis."

"Thank you." At first sight the coffee seems a bit too watered down. The cup is almost filled up all the way to the brim. I know I asked for a double espresso *corretto*, but still. I take a sip. Giacomino has put a generous pour of grappa in it. I glance over to him.

"My pleasure," he says and starts off.

"Say?"

"What's that, sir?"

"Do you happen to know if there's something going on in the church?"

"Sunday mass."

"When? Now?"

"In about half-hour ... That reminds me. I'd better go get ready. It will be quite hectic around here in a little bit."

"How come? A lot of people attending?"

"Only the whole town."

"All right, don't let me keep you ... Oh, wait! How much do I owe you?"

"It'll be my pleasure."

"What? No, I insist."

"Please!"

"Thank you, Giacomino." He nods and smiles then walks away.

Given the youngster's hyperbolic nature, I don't take him too seriously; however, soon enough, fifteen to twenty minutes' time the most, Giacomino proves me wrong. He didn't exaggerate at all, quite the contrary. It's as if the entire town, rising from the depths of slumber, has suddenly gotten on its feet. From each of the capillary streets branching out from the piazza, waves of villagers all dressed to the nines come surging forward. For a good while there, the stream of townspeople carries on uninterrupted, seemingly unstoppable. Then as abruptly as it started the influx of dwellers pouring into the square dies off.

For about five to ten minutes, the earlier stillness and quietude of the indolent morning give way to the utmost chaos: young kids, scampering; toddlers, all buckled up in strollers, crying and screaming; men, having full conversations by shouting at each other from opposite sides of the square. Giacomino was also absolutely right about getting ready for it. Large numbers of people flood the bars trying to grab, I'm assuming, a quick coffee before mass. And who could blame them. If it's the same priest as yesterday officiating, I'd need a whole thermos of coffee to stay awake.

The basilica's splayed portal opens. With a sedate but steady movement, the masses of residents proceed to it. As they slowly disappear inside the basilica, the incessant clamour tapers off, and peace and quiet reign supreme again. The three-tier loggia must be bursting at the seams right now. It looks to me that was even more people than at the funeral. Perhaps, I'm wrong.

"May I?"

"What? ... Oh, yes. Go ahead." Giacomino takes the empty cup from the table and throws it on a tray he's holding with his left hand. "You weren't kidding."

"What's that, Mr. De Angelis?"

"The people. You weren't joking about how hectic it gets."

"Oh ... That ... "

"Is it always like this?"

"On Sundays? Yes. Well, unless it's raining. I don't recall who said it but ... 'Rain is anti-revolutionary!' Or something along those lines."

"How old are you, Giacomino? If you don't mind my asking."

"Fourteen."

"Fourteen!" The soul of a wise man trapped in a teenager's body.

"Would you accept another one?"

"No, thank you."

He bows as a way of farewell. I watch him walk away.

Out of the corner of my eye, I catch sight of some latecomers. I can't make them out at first, but once they get close enough, I recognize them. It's Tommasini's family. I swiftly, yet nonchalantly, turn my chair so as to face the bar's storefront, hoping to remain unseen. It works. I follow them with a sideway look until they disappear inside the basilica. Facing back at the bar, I spot Giacomino up on the door sill, leaning with his left shoulder on the entrance's marbled jamb, his hands stuffed in his pockets, his left foot crossed over the other, his brow knitted. I draw his attention with a chin tilt. He bolts over.

"I think I'll take you up on that offer if it still stands."

"Of course! Same?"

"Same, thank you."

This cup of coffee is just as full as the previous one. I turn my chair to face the piazza again. Ten to fifteen minutes pass before I see one of the church's secondary doors on the right side of the splayed portal open. From it, a flock of kids, giggling and shushing each other, come stealing out. They quickly disperse and regroup in the middle of the piazza, by the bust of Garibaldi. They all hunch in a circle, scheming something. Within a minute or two, one of the secondary entrances of the church opens again, slowly revealing Marinella. She joins the rest of the kids, who make room for her to get in the circle. They stay in that position a while longer, still plotting something.

The circle finally breaks up. The boys, leading the way, start running southwards. The girls follow in their trail. At the end of the square, I see them all turning right. It looks like they're going to the belvedere. I remain seated a trice longer then spring to my feet. Before taking off, however, I turn around, searching for Giacomino. I want to thank him again, but I don't see him. He must be inside. No matter. I set off across the piazza in the direction of the terrace. To get there, I choose a different route than the one taken by the kids. It's a little more convoluted but should lead me to it all the same.

Three porticos and several flights of stairs later, I reach the belvedere. My inkling was correct. The kids are all gathered by the south-facing terrace. I sidle to a bench behind a giant municipal planter, which is close enough to be able to see the kids and hear what they are saying quite clearly, but not so close as to be seen. From where I'm sitting, it seems as though the boys, devilishly incited by the girls, are daring each other to walk on top of the low and narrow parapet.

One of them — the shorter and huskier one, who is clearly not at the centre of the girls' attention — rises to the challenge. They all go quiet for a moment. The expressions plastered on their faces are that of astonishment, especially on those of the more popular boys, who, I bet, had not predicted such an outcome. Suddenly all the girls, but Marinella, go wild: screaming and laughing with excitement, teasing the other boys by questioning their prowess. Eventually, the girls channel their euphoria into a drilling chant: "Go! Go! Go!"

They all move aside to give the heavy-set boy some room. He takes his Sunday jacket off, folds it neatly, and hands it over to one of the girls, who is now showering him with attention. The other boys simply stand there watching, their faces livid. He unbuttons his shirtsleeves and rolls them up with great care. Judging by the overly meticulous procedure, it's fairly obvious he's trying to buy some time. He must be cursing at his misguided burst of manhood. He's ready; it appears. He walks to the parapet and rests his hands on it, but before climbing on it he turns around one more time. An icy smile splits his rotund face in half.

The chanting grows louder, and up he goes. The climb, clumsy and awkward, prompts some laughs. He's standing there nearly unable to hold himself up, his face the colour of magma. In an attempt to stop the giggling, I'm assuming, and perhaps to reclaim the attention of the girls, he finds the strength to steady himself, and to the surprise of everybody he pulls an impressive, as per the girls' reaction to it, stunt. Emulating some kind of karate move, he stands on the parapet on one foot, his arms lifted well above his head, his hands cupped like the paws of an animal.

It occurs to me that the kids' horsing around has become a little too hazardous. If the fat kid were to fall on the wrong side of that parapet, it'd be a sure and horrible death. I have to intervene.

"You'd better get off before you get hurt," I say, getting up. The kids freeze. Their petrified expressions tell me they had no idea I was sitting here. The plump boy's brazenness of seconds ago gives way to sudden unsureness, to the point that I see him dangerously wobbling. Perhaps, I shouldn't have said anything. "Don't look the other way and, please, do not look down!" All the kids turn their terrified stares to the trembling boy on the parapet. "It's all right. There's nothing to worry about, okay?" I say, advancing toward him. "Listen to my voice. Now, slowly, put your other leg down ... Yes, like that ... Nice and easy ... See, that's easy ... "

I'm lying through my teeth. The boy is panicking. He's so shaky right now I seriously fear he might fall. I'm walking fast, but not so fast to make him even more nervous. The kids' eyes well up. While most of the boys manage to hold their tears back, the girls burst into an uncontrollable cry. I signal to them to hold back so as not to scare the boy on the wall. It's no use. There's no time left; the boy is about to pass out. I make a sprint for it.

I catch him just in time.

I lower him to the ground and give him a couple of slaps on the face.

"That was extraordinary," a voice, coming from behind, says. I turn to it. "*Gesù mio*! ... I was passing by when I saw him on the wall ... The way he was trembling, I thought he was going to fall ... *Gesù, Gesù, Gesù*! ... Do you see what could've happened if this brave man wasn't here? Do you?" Except for Marinella, the kids are still bawling. The man shakes his head dramatically from side to side, muttering some kind of verses. "How is he?" he asks at the end of his soliloquy.

"I don't know." I'm about to give him another slap on the face when I see him moving. He moans something. His face is white as chalk, as if life has been drained out of his body.

The boy regains his senses. As soon as realizes he's lying on the ground, he bounces to his feet, pretending like nothing happened.

"You all right?" I ask.

"Yes, of course. Why do you ask? ... I wanted to scare them," he says, letting out a strained cackle.

Though understandable, his attempt to save face in the eyes of the girls doesn't produce a favourable outcome. In fact, none of the other youngsters, whose facial expressions have now shifted from terror to scorn, seem to buy his story, and amid a landslide of taunts they set off to the square. The fat boy trails in their wake. Marinella stays behind.

"Kids!" the passer-by says, still shaking his head, and with no longer a reason to be here. He strikes me as the chatty type. I don't want to encourage him, so I don't say anything. A snorted chuckle and a shoulder shrug are all I offer him. He seems to get the message. "Well, then," he says, doffing his cap. "I hope you have a pleasant day, Mr. ... "

"I hope you have a pleasant day as well." He puts his cap back on his glossy dome and snails away.

The second the man walks out of view, I turn to Marinella. She's not there anymore. I look about me and sight her behind the big planter. She's climbed on the same bench I was sitting on before. I hesitate a moment then move toward her. From under her knitted brow, she follows me with her eyes. I'm standing next to her now, silent, barely able to hold or decipher for that matter her elliptical gaze. Sure, I see sorrow and anger, but I can fathom far, far more to it. I'm perfectly still, yet I feel as though every muscle in my body is giving a violent lurch. Before long, however, these internal spasms give way to a sensation of utter drainage, a general but total collapse. I can hardly stand on my own two feet right now. As whatever is left of my strength seeps, inexorably, out of my body, a fog, like a thin layer of tightly woven fibrous threads, descends over my eyes. My knees buckle. I must sit down.

"Can I?" I manage to say, pointing at the bench.

Marinella doesn't say anything. She moves slightly, as though to make room for me to sit, even if there already is plenty of space on the bench. I plump down on it, though I don't mean to. She, perhaps a touch defensively, immediately draws her legs to her chest, perching her crossed arms on top of her knees, and letting her head rest sideways over her arms. Her luscious, billowing ringlets cascade all to one side, exposing her long neck, sinuously stretching from her shoulders to her seashell ears, where it gently fades to resurface as a dainty jawline, contouring her oval porcelain face, which radiates grace and beauty suggestive of past centuries.

There must be something brewing in her head, for her rouged, cupid's bow lips pucker up, and her crystalline stare gradually takes on a greyish hue while shifting inwardly, withdrawing, it seems to me, to remote places; a sombre veil pulls over her face. I scour my brain for something to say, anything at all, but my head is filled with a horde of jumbled thoughts. The more I keep at it, the more they muddle up; to the extent that I find myself estranged from my surroundings.

All of a sudden, I'm terrifyingly conscious of the inner workings of my body. I can feel each movement, palpitation, spasm; I can hear every click, rustle, swoosh; I can sense each and every blood vessel, nerve ending, muscle tissue. My teeth are grinding. An unendurable urge to peel off my skin and scream leaves me no choice but to stand up at once.

Same as a crazed caged creature, I pace in a circle, pressing down on my brow we both palms of my hands. My jaw is clenched so tight my temples bulge out. I'm beginning to feel dizzy. I take the palms away from my forehead. It's too late. It's as if I'm inside a centrifuge and can't stop the spinning. I reach for something to hold on to, but with nothing immediately around me, I inevitably tumble to the ground, flailing my arms and legs like a measly crawler hopelessly flipped onto its back. I eventually manage to get on my hands and knees and stay like that, waiting for the world to stop swirling.

As things slowly begin settling down, I attempt to lift myself up, but a surging nausea anchors me to the ground. It's so sudden and so powerful I'm afraid to so much as blink. I try to fight it. It's futile. My whole body is being dragged down as though by a formidable undertow, solely to be thrust back forward with great virulence. Gushes of vomit spew out of my mouth. There's nothing but bile remaining, yet my stomach heaves.

As the contractions finally stop and a sense of relief sets in, I reach for my kerchief and wipe my mouth with it. I'm still on my hands and knees when, without warning, I feel the touch of a tiny hand gently stroking my nape. The mere contact makes me jolt. My skin curls up. She does it again. This time as soon as her hand brushes against my skin ripples of shooting pain quickly spread to every part of my body. I can feel the nausea swelling up again.

Instantly, I flip myself around and, as a reflex, grab Marinella's hand. I must be squeezing it a little too hard, for Marinella's face warps as if in pain. Her figure contorts to one side. Her imploring eyes seek mine. I let go of her hand. She swiftly steps back, rubbing her right wrist with her left hand. A look like that of someone who's been woundingly betrayed crops up on her face. A few disjointed syllables escape my mouth, but I don't think they add up to anything coherent. Though still weak, I rise to my feet. She's still looking at me with the same look on her face, only more severe. I run away.

* * *

The child is far behind me and completely out of sight, but I'm still running, and for some reason I don't stop until I reach the wall shrine atop the village. I'm utterly depleted. Not one ounce of strength is left in my body. Were it not for a garbage can I make use of to prop myself up, I would fold to the ground in an instant. I close my eyes to replenish somehow. I'm not sure for how long I stay like that. It's the buzzing sound of a three-wheeler getting close that makes me realize I've drifted. By the time I look over at the vehicle, it draws up a few metres from me. Because of the angle of the sun, I can't see who the driver is. The faded-sage three-wheeler wobbles slightly, and the door screeches opens. It's Turiddu. I'm not sure what he's doing here, or what he wants. He hurriedly lights up a cigarette and strides toward me.

"You're in big trouble, Mr. De Angelis!"

"How did you find me here?"

"Let's just say I had an inkling ... Anyway, it doesn't matter."

"What do you want?"

"Didn't you here what I said? ... You're in big trouble!"

"How do you mean?"

"They're looking for you—"

"Who's *they*?"

"Alfio, *in primis*. You know Tommasini's brother-in-law? ... But he's not the only one, that's for sure."

"Why are they looking for me exactly?"

"Why? ... What happened at the belvedere?"

"I'm not following—"

"Really? ... The kids are saying some weird things though—"

"Weird how?"

"Well, one of them said you almost made him fall in the canyon ... And that you touched him? ... You wouldn't let him up or something?"

"I was trying to help him—"

"Is that right? ... And what about Marinella? Tommasini's daughter?"

"What about her?"

"She was quite shaken up ... She said you grabbed her arm? ... To be fair, she wasn't making much sense, but still ... As I said she was quite shaken up ... Look, let's be honest here. You don't have much time. They're gonna look everywhere for you. It's a matter of time before they find you here. I'm telling you. They won't stop until they catch you. They'll scour every nook and cranny if necessary. You gotta listen to me ... You'd better leave this place as soon as possible ... Of course, it's a bit tricky now. You can't go back to my cousin's house. That's the first place they'll check. You might have to lay low till it gets dark and then get the hell outta here."

"How do you propose I do that?"

"Well ... If I were you, I'd hide inside the abandoned building. You *know* the one I'm talking about."

"Wouldn't they look in there too?"

"Of course! ... Not *every* room ... Enough said?"

"Why are you doing this?"

"What am I doing?"

"Why are you trying to help me all of a sudden? What's with the big reversal? ... Last night you were threatening me!"

"Look, I get it. You're sceptical. It's totally understandable. I know how it looks ... But lemme say one more thing ... I know ... I *know* what you're going through ... Good enough?" I don't say anything. "We'd better get outta here." Turiddu throws the half-smoked cigarette on the ground and marches back to the three-wheeler. I follow him. "This is what we'll do. You hop in the back and pull the tarpaulin over you. And do not, under no circumstances, move. Not until we arrive. I'll take you to the rear of the building. It's safer that way. I'll give you a signal: two knocks. Questions?" I shake my head. "All right … Let's get a move on before someone sees us."

I do as he instructs, even though I don't believe a single word he's saying. I don't know why. I should avoid him like the plague, but instead I climb onto the flatbed and slide under the tarpaulin. A few seconds later, we're speeding downhill. It's only after many a sudden turn and far too many potholes that the three-wheeler comes to a complete stop. Two knocks. That's the signal. I slide out from under the tarpaulin and climb down the flatbed. My feet have narrowly touched the ground, and Turiddu is already driving away. The houses on this side of the building are sparser, and some of them inhabited it seems. I can see why he wanted to drop me off here. With my back up against the wall, I stealthily shoulder around the construction. There's not a soul around as far as I can tell. It's now or never. I walk to the corrugated-metal sheet, lift it, and slip inside the building.

I cautiously cross the dingy ground floor, making sure there's no one but me inside, and just as cautiously go up the stairs. All clear. On the top floor, I peek outside the balcony, careful not to be seen. Swiftly, I jump onto it, rush to the boarded-up window, and squeeze myself inside the sealed room. I stay put for a moment to allow my eyes to adjust to the dim lighting. When I'm finally able to distinguish forms, shapes and a certain degree of details, I move to the crate by the dust cloth. I sit there staring at the rectangular, sun-framed window.

The high contrast almost instantly causes me to lose perception of any fine details. Everything within and immediately around the sun-framed window meshes into a black mass. The more I stare at it, the more it deepens. So gaping and unfathomable, in fact, it takes on an oppressive and somewhat frightening quality. My sight becomes fuzzy and ultimately turns into double vision. I look away. Unwittingly, like a child's way of keeping the growing darkness at bay, my limbs draw closer to my body; my back hunches; my neck sinks into my shoulders.

I hear a noise, a thud. A series of shushing sounds follow. They're here already. I keep quiet, absolutely still. Within a few seconds, I can clearly distinguish the sound of steps, racing up the stairs. There are several of them. How many exactly, it's hard to tell. They've reached the top floor. I can tell by the abrupt, conspicuous silence. I shut my eyes and bring my index as well as my middle finger to my right ear and press down on it. I can almost see and hear them gesturing to each other. It doesn't take long for them to start moving again. It sounds like they're spreading. Some of them step away from the room I'm in, and some others seem to come closer; meanwhile, not a single word is spoken. They stop again.

A voice breaks the silence. "There's nobody here."

"Here too," another voice says, from farther away.

"Same here," yet another echoes, even farther.

"Where the hell is he?" someone else shouts. His timbre of voice reminds me of Alfio's.

"Wait a minute. Did you hear that?" I could be wrong, but I'm pretty certain that's Turiddu's voice.

"What are you talking about? I didn't hear anything," the voice says. No room for doubt this time. It's definitely Alfio's voice.

"That noise!"

"What noise?"

"I heard something moving in there."

"In there? You sure?"

"On my mother's eyes ... I swear I heard something in there."

They must be talking about this room, the one I'm in. As far as I can remember, there aren't any other closed off rooms.

"All right ... Come here everybody. You, gimme that ...Yes, that ... Come on hurry up!" Footsteps marching toward me dispel any doubt. They *are* talking about this room. I stay still nonetheless.

A sudden loud thud catches me off guard. Another even louder thump makes the whole room quake. An eerie silence, interrupted only by the sound of crumbling debris, follows. My whole body is tensed up. I hold my breath for God knows how long, waiting for the inevitable. And even though I know it's coming, I jolt all the same when the thumping resumes. It's more violent and faster this time, as if driven by a single-minded determination. I can barely see it, but I can definitely taste the dust rising from the debris. The maddening percussion goes on relentlessly; thud after thud is all I can hear now; and with every additional blow, I can feel the vibrations reaching deeper and deeper down in my bones.

One of the airbricks on the top row of the door falls off, smashing to the floor and leaving a sizeable opening behind.

"You ... Come here ... Gimme a hand." I can hear them moving about. Once they settle, a couple of probing hands appear in the hole. "Ready? Go!" And with a grunt, Alfio's face crops up in the opening. His eyes flutter. He hasn't spotted me yet. He sticks his head in a bit. I can see him now squinting in my direction. I don't move, even though I'm certain he's found me. He doesn't say anything or move. He simply stares at me.

"Is he in there?" a voice asks.

Alfio withdraws his head from the opening and glances down at the person who's holding him up. "Lemme down." He disappears behind the bricks.

I don't know what they are doing. They are not talking or moving. The morose and extremely loud silence is asphyxiating.

They start hammering again.

Blow after blow, I watch the bricks shatter to the floor, the opening getting wider and wider. By the time they stop banging, there's but the bottom row left. Alfio, holding a sledgehammer, Turiddu, and some other faces I don't recognize stand by the door, looking in.

Chapter Twenty

"**What about here?**" asks the doctor, pressing down with the palm of his right hand on the upper left side of my chest.

"No."

He moves his hand a little lower. "And here?"

"Yes."

"Yes?"

"Yes, I said yes!"

"Is it minor discomfort or—"

"It hurts. Stop touching it!"

"Sorry."

"No, *I'm* sorry … It's … very painful, that's all. It feels like someone is sticking a knife in it."

"I see."

The phone rings. The doctor doesn't seem to pay attention to it. He's still probing, this time a little more gently, my left side with his right hand. The phone keeps ringing.

"My sister will get that," he says, answering my wondering gaze. It rings again. "Concetta! ... The phone!" he bellows. The ringing finally stops.

"Do you know how I got here?"

"The *Brigadiere* ... He brought you here. He's still outside."

"The *Brigadiere*?"

"Uh huh ... "

"Was I out for long?"

"No, not long ... If you don't mind my asking? What happened?"

"He didn't say?"

"Who? The *Brigadiere*? To me? ... Not a word!" I writhe in pain. "What is it?"

"My jaw. I can barely talk ... "

"Well, that's natural. It's really badly bruised. The good news is I don't think it's fractured ... Maybe a mild fissure ... Of course, I can't be one hundred percent sure. You'll have to have it x-rayed to confirm ... On the other hand, I'm pretty certain you have a couple of broken ribs. But, again, an x-ray is the best way to verify that. I'd recommend you do that as soon as possible. I'd do it myself, but we're not equipped here."

"I see."

"All in all— " There's a rap at the door. "Excuse me. Come in." The doctor's sister timidly appears from behind the door.

"Alfonso," she calls out with that peculiar vibrato of hers, her complexion pastier than ever.

"What is it?" She hesitates answering. "Oh, Mr. De

Angelis, you remember my sister?" I nod. "So, what is it?"
She stands there stooped like a lamppost, her lips as though
sutured. Her body contorts in the most awkward way.
"What's the matter with you? You having a stroke or something?"

"Alfonso!" she cries out, storming out of the room.

"Good! Run! ... I can't bear the sight of her anymore!
... You know I will never, *ever*, be able to get rid of her ...
I'm stuck with that repugnant, noisome old bat! ... I oughta
throw her in a dungeon and hose her down! ... Anyway ...
I'd better go see what she wants."

I can hear them arguing in the hallway. Suddenly their
voices go down to a whisper. This goes on for a couple of
minutes or so; then, the doctor comes back in, his demeanour
entirely changed. He comes over to me with great reluctance.

"So ... Where were we? ... Um ... Oh ..." He turns to a
cabinet, off to the side, and reaches for some boxes. "Here,
these should give you some relief. However, don't take them
for an extended period of time, and ... I cannot stress this
enough, do not ingest more than one pill at a time. It's also
preferable you eat something prior to taking it ... Questions?" I shake my head. "All right, you can get dressed
now. Let me know if you need any help with that."

"Thank you. I'll be all right."

The doctor steps out of the room again. I start putting
my shirt on, but it turns out to be not an easy task. I can
hardly bend my torso. Even the slightest of movements
causes great pain. I finally manage to get my shirt buttoned
up and reach for my pants. As I'm about to slip them on, I
hear the doorbell ring. By the time I'm tightening the belt,
the door opens, revealing the doctor and, looming directly

behind him, the *Maresciallo* immediately followed by the *Brigadiere*.

"Is there anything I can fetch you? … Coffee? … Almond cookies, perhaps?"

"No thank you," the *Maresciallo* says. "We need to talk to Mr. De Angelis here."

"Oh yes, of course. I'll get out of your hair."

The moment the doctor shuts the door behind him, the *Maresciallo* ominously rotates his colossal figure toward me, his beetling brow heavily crinkled. He picks up a chair and sits across from where I'm sitting, staring at me square in the eyes. His gaze is so menacing, I can barely hold it. He doesn't move, not even to blink. I'm not sure what he's waiting for. All the same, I think it best not to say anything for the moment.

"What do you have to say for yourself?" the *Brigadiere* says suddenly. Even the *Maresciallo* seems surprised by the underling's outburst. "What kind of excuse do you have this time? Huh?" I keep quiet. "Nothing? … You can't think of anything? Too little time to make one up? … It doesn't matter 'cause there's nothing—*nothing*, you hear me?—nothing you can say that's gonna get you outta this! You piece of shit—"

"Enough!" the *Maresciallo* bellows.

"What?" the *Brigadiere* says, dumbfounded.

"Lemme talk to Mr. De Angelis alone."

"But—"

"That's an order! … Get the hell outta here right now! … I am not gonna say it again." Fuming with rage, the *Brigadiere* flounces out of the doctor's office, slamming the door with such violence it makes the whole room shudder.

"Please, forgive him. He's a little emotional about this. Of course, it's understandable given the circumstances. Don't you think?"

"What circumstances?"

"What did I say to you this morning?"

"You said a lot of things."

"Feel free to correct me if I'm wrong. Didn't I say to you that I did not want to see you again?" I don't say anything. "And yet, here we are ... You had many a chance to leave this place ... *Many* ... You've been a thorn in my side ever since you got here, before even ... I could've never, ever imagined that this was your end game all along and —you know what?—still can't ... "

"What are you talking about?"

"Don't pretend like you don't know what I'm talking about. It's not gonna work. You disgust me! What the hell were you doing with those kids?"

"I'm not sure what you mean."

"Really? ... Are you in pain?" I nod. "Good! ... Now, as much as I'd like to beat the living shit out of you right this second, I do have a problem ... And, please, make no mistake: I don't give two shits about you. For all I care, I'd throw you back on the street and let them finish the job. Just so we're clear. But here's my ... problem, shall we say? ... Maybe you can help me figure this out ... That closed-off room they found you in ... You see ... I can't wrap my head around it ... *That* is my problem."

"I'm not following."

"All right ... Lemme put it this way ... The bricks closing off the door to that sick room were not laid by contractors. Someone else did it ... "

"I didn't do it—"

"Lemme finish. I checked every centimetre of that place, every piece of dust, everything. The work on the wall ... The hole ... The receptacle ... They're older than a week, no doubt. Months I'd say, if not more. So, no, you didn't do that ... That's pretty obvious to me. But here's my problem ... How did you find that room? How did you know how to get in there? I mean, how did you know you could access it through the window, which, by the way, is not even visible from the inside." The doorbell rings again. "That's extraordinary, isn't it? It's like you have some kinda ... sixth sense, shall we say? ... Care to venture an explanation, Mr. De Angelis?"

The door to the doctor's office flings wide open. It's the young *Appuntato*. "*Maresciallo*!" he cries out, catching his breath.

"What the hell is going on here! ... How dare you storming in here like this! ... Where's the *Brigadiere*?"

"I'm here." He materializes from behind the young *Appuntato*.

"Explain!"

"The *Appuntato* here says he's got something important to report. Apparently, it can't wait."

"*I* say what *can* or *cannot* wait, is that understood? This is gonna have to wait ... Now, clear the room. Both of you! And you"—addressing the *Appuntato*—"we're gonna have a little chat."

"But *Maresciallo*," the *Appuntato* says, "there's a witness!"

"A what?"

"A witness."

Stunned by the new development, the *Maresciallo* falls silent for a moment. "Let's take this outside."

They all step into the hallway. I can't really hear what they are saying; their voices are too low. Not a lot of time passes, though, before the *Maresciallo* comes back inside, shutting the door behind him with a slow guided gesture, almost as if not wanting to let go of the doorknob. He lingers there for a moment, cloaked in an air of pensiveness, which is making his beetling brow protrude even more. Then, same as coming out of a daydream, he looks up at me. Visibly reluctant, he lets go of the doorknob, falters to the chair he was sitting in, and, literally, plumps on it deep in thought. He remains in that state for what seems an eternity. It probably appears so because of the excruciating pain I'm experiencing right now. I'm barely capable of sitting up. All the same, I decide to stay silent and leave it to him to utter the first word.

He changes sitting position and takes a deep, long breath, which makes his herculean chest swell up. "Well … What can I say, Mr. De Angelis? Just when I thought I had you pegged! … I'm afraid an apology is in order."

"What do you mean?"

"As the *Appuntato* mentioned before, there's a witness … Evidently, you're a hero!"

"I beg your pardon?"

"My thoughts precisely … It would appear that a certain Prof. Gaetano Angirillo saw the whole thing. According to his colourful account of the events that took place at the terrace, you actually saved the boy's life, contrarily to what that little shit said."

Taking a folded piece of paper out of his pocket, he goes on to say: "And I quote: 'I was, as per my usual at this glorious hour of the morning, perambulating through the belvedere when I caught a glimpse of this young boy in peril, up on the parapet. His step struck me as dangerously unsound. I must confess. For the most dreadful of moments, I stood by, fearing the worst. And just as I thought no more could be done for this young, precious boy, a pale stranger, out of a clear blue sky, launches himself forward with a formidable Olympian thewy, saving the boy's life.' I'll spare you the part where he compares you to several Greek gods. I didn't even know there were that many ... Well, Mr. De Angelis, what can I say?"

"You couldn't possibly know."

"That's very big of you ... I wonder though why Marinella said that you grabbed her arm ... "

"I ... don't know."

"I suppose she could've lied too. In any case ... I have to ask: if you wish, you have the right to file charges against your assailers — "

"No. I'm not going to do that."

"Good. That's a wise decision."

"Now what?"

"That's a good question ... We can't possibly let you outta here alone. It's not safe for you yet ... Tell you what. We'll take you to your lodging, so you can gather all your stuff. And then we'll take you to the bus station. If I'm not mistaken, there's a coach leaving for Palermo within the hour. You should be able to make it. Questions?"

"No."

"Can you walk?"

"I think so."

"All right. Whenever you're ready, Mr. De Angelis."

* * *

Walking down the hallway towards the exit, I can already tell by the clamour trickling in from outside that a mob of people crowds the entrance to the doctor's house, itching to put their hands on me.

"Wait here," the *Maresciallo* says, as we approach the door. He opens it cautiously. A thick wall of angry people fully blocks the way. "Everybody! ... Step back! ... You hear me? ... I'm not gonna say it again, all of you move!"

Though markedly hesitant, the throng of inveighing villagers slowly splits in the middle, clearing the way enough for us to pass, but not enough, at least as far as I'm concerned, to feel comfortable, or safe for that matter, parading through it.

The *Brigadiere*, standing right behind me, gives me a slight push and says: "Let's go."

It's not a long walk by any stretch, but it's extremely hard to ignore the deep-seated disgust pencilled over their faces, the fulminating stares, all the mouths curled in contempt—loaded with spit, and ready to spew it. Fortunately, we make it to the armoured jeep without further incident, and as soon as the *Appuntato*, who's the last one to get on the vehicle, slams the door, we drive away with the siren blasting and at the speed of a high-risk car chase, like the ones you see in American movies.

* * *

There's no one at the lodging. No one in front of it. No one within a few-block radius. The *Maresciallo* and the *Brigadiere* stay put, to guard the entrance, I suppose, while the young *Appuntato* and I step inside the house. It looks like Teresa is still out.

"Where's your stuff?" he asks. I point at the ceiling. "Upstairs?"

"Last floor."

The *Appuntato* is a kind young fellow. He volunteers to go up to my room and gather my belongings for me. As he darts up the stairs, I drag myself to the kitchen, take out some stationery out of the drawer, and quickly draft a message for Teresa. By the time I finish penning it, I can already hear the *Appuntato* avalanche down the stairs.

"Mr. De Angelis," he calls out.

"In here."

"Where?"

"The kitchen ... That was fast!"

"I don't want the *Maresciallo* to wait for too long." He leans forward, assuming the posture of someone who's about to whisper. "Between us, he's not exactly the patient kind. If you know what I mean?"

It couldn't be any clearer, but I indulge him anyway. "Is he?"

"You bet! ... You ready? What's that you're holding?"

"This? ... Oh, nothing ... It's a message for Teresa. The landlady?"

"I'm not sure this is ... Maybe I should go out and ask—"

"It's just an apology!" I swiftly add, appealing to his kindness.

For a moment, I can see him struggling, quite visibly, between his sense of duty and his good-natured inclination. He cedes to my plea. "Fine," he says. I perceive regret in his voice. "Let's go."

I drop the note in the middle of the table and follow him.

* * *

At the new quarter, the bus to Palermo is already in the departure lane, with both the door and the luggage compartment wide open. The *Maresciallo* escorts me to the coach.

"Here we are, Mr. De Angelis ... I'd say that all in all it was a pretty good visit!" I don't say anything. "You know ... There's something that's still ... bothering me, shall we say? I can't put my finger on it ... *Why* were you hiding? I mean, if you didn't do anything! ... You see ... It's as if you ... knew, shall we say? ... that the kids would lie about it. Almost as if you knew they were looking for you. And how's that possible? ... But that's not the only thing that's bothering me, you see? ... You were spotted going towards the wall shrine. That's at the opposite side of the village! And, unless I got the timeline completely wrong, they were already looking for you. And I mean everywhere. You see? ... How the hell did you manage to walk all the way back to the abandoned building without being seen? ... No offence, but with your complexion you're not exactly ... easy to miss, shall we say?"

The bus driver steps outside. "Are you boarding this bus?" he asks.

"He is," the *Maresciallo* says. "Step back inside." It looks like the driver wouldn't even dream of arguing with him, for he hops back on the bus so fast he almost breaks his front teeth, tripping on the last step. "So ... Care to explain?"

"You're asking the wrong questions."

"What do you mean?"

"How did they find me in there?"

The *Maresciallo*'s eyes narrow. His lips move, but not a sound comes out of them. He stands motionless, as though to allow what I said to sink in. I leave him there ruminating and slowly get on the bus. From the corner of my eye, I can see he's still trying to figure out what I meant. He follows me, as I walk down the aisle to find a seat. The bus takes off even before I can sit down.

* * *

"Montanari's residence."

"Hello?"

"Yes, hello?"

"Sorry. The connection is a bit shaky, and it's quite noisy in here. This is De Angeli—"

"Please, wait. I'll get Mr. Montanari on the phone."

"Thank you."

"Hello? De Angelis?"

"Yes."

"It's funny you called. I was debating whether to call *you*."

"How come?"

"I received a really weird phone call from the *Maresciallo* early this morning."

"Weird how?"

"I don't know. He wanted to confirm some details about the 'timeline' he called it, which I thought was strange, considering you said everything was settled. I asked him if there was something the matter. He said no. Just routine questions, he said ... And ... Oh ... He also wanted to know when you were leaving town. I told him I didn't know exactly. It depended on how long it took to finalize the transaction. He kind of hung up on me after that. Anyway ... What's going on? I thought we said you were going to call me tomorrow. Am I wrong?"

"No. That's right."

"So? What is it?"

"I'm afraid I have bad news."

"Shit! I knew it ... What happened?"

"Look ... I have to tell you the truth ... The deal's been dead for a while now."

"What? ... I don't understand."

"The Colantonio brothers let me know almost right away they were not interested in moving forward with the deal."

"Why didn't you tell me?"

"I thought I could get them to change their minds, but ... I was mistaken."

"I see."

"So, yes. That's why I didn't tell you anything right away. I know it was stupid ... It's impossible to deal with these people."

"I'm beginning to get an idea. Still … I wish you had told me … I suppose I have to appreciate your trying. Where are you? I hear a lot of background noise."

"I'm at the train station in Palermo."

"You're on your way back already?"

"Actually … I was going to ask you for some time off if that's okay."

"Oh … You mean now?"

"Yes."

"Well, I wish you'd given me a little more notice … How much time do you need?"

"I don't know yet."

"Are you all right?"

"I'm fine. I need some time off. That's all."

"All right … Um … No problem. Take all the time you need. You set for money?"

"I'm good."

"You sure? You know what? I'll wire you some."

"That's not necessary."

"I insist."

"Thank you."

"So … "

"What?"

"Are you going to tell me where you're going?"

"I don't know yet. I'll play it by ear."

"You?" I don't say anything. "Okay then … I guess I'll see you when you get here, whenever that is … Have fun, I suppose."

The pain in my ribs flares up. Without a moment's thought, I hang up the receiver. I stand there by the pay phone, waiting for the throbbing to subside. As the discomfort drops to a more manageable level, I reach for my luggage and trudge out of the train station terminal.

* * *

"*Stazione di* Colasberta," the bus driver announces, as the coach draws up to the sheltered platform. "*Stazione di* Colasberta," he repeats. "This is a brief stop, so if you need to get off, do so quickly. Thank you ... Colasberta ... *Stazione di* Colasberta ... Anybody getting off?"

"I am."

"Do you have any luggage, sir?"

"Yes."

He quickly steps out of the bus. I follow him.

"Which one is your luggage?"

"That one."

"This?"

"Yes. Thank you."

The driver fetches it and literally throws it at me. I move sideways to avoid impact. The luggage flies by me, landing on the other side of the platform. He looks at me stupefied. "Why didn't you catch it?"

"I would've if I'd known you were going to throw it at me."

He seems puzzled by my response but doesn't say a word. He simply slams the storage compartment and climbs back on the bus. Within seconds, the coach drives away.

I cross the parking lot/bus terminal to the waiting room inside the station. It's empty. I walk to the ticket booth. There's no one behind the glass screen. I wait there a while, but nobody shows up. I knock on the glass. Still, nothing.

I knock again. A door in the back of the booth angles open. A head quickly protrudes from behind it and just as quickly recedes. The door opens wider, revealing the toothless employee. He's as unctuous and as shabby as I remembered him. I don't think he's recognized me yet, perhaps because of all the bruises on my face. He shuts the door behind him and quicksteps to the glass screen. He's about to say something but stops short of it when he finally realizes who I am.

"Do you have a locker?" I ask him. He stares at me blankly. "A locker? Do you have one?" He nods emphatically, as if suddenly grasping what I'm talking about, and stoops to get something. He comes back up holding a dusty, laminated piece of cardboard. He blows on it and shows it to me. It's a price list for the locker. "That's fine." The employee moves away from the glass and comes out of the booth. Without saying a single word, he walks toward me, lifts up my luggage, and takes it somewhere past the ticket booth. I wait there.

Not even a minute later, he shows up again, bouncing all the way to me. He extends his right arm and hands me a round metal tag with a number on it. The second I take it off his hand, he swivels back and starts off. "Wait!" He stops in mid-stride and looks at me. I signal him to come closer. Though sceptical, judging by his body language, he obliges me. He stands there, looking up, perhaps a little closer than I wanted him to—his breath as rotten as ever. I reach for my jacket pocket and take out an envelope filled with money. I'm not even sure how much in it exactly. I hand it to him. He seems confused by it. So much so that he's hesitant in accepting it and takes a step backward.

"It's all right. Take it … This is for you. Take it." He gets closer again and motions for the envelope. Cautiously, he peeks inside it. His face lights up. "Was I ever here?" He nods even more emphatically than before and flails his hands in the air. "Do you understand what I'm saying to you?"

He beats his chest resoundingly with his fist and intones: "*Mutu, orbu, e surdu sugnu!*"

"I take that as a yes."

Acknowledgements

Thank you to the instructors and staff at the University of Toronto School of Continuing Studies Creative Writing Department, especially Catherine Graham, Ibi Kaslik, Rabindranath Maharaj, Ken Murray, Alexandra Leggat, Ray Robertson, Thom Vernon, and Marina Nemat. An extra handshake to Lee Gowan just for being Lee Gowan. To my teacher and mentor Michel Basilières, to whom I'm forever indebted, for extending so much in the way of support, opportunity, and warmth. Without his guidance and encouragement, this novel would not exist. To Dejan Radic for his stunning artwork, gracing the cover. To David Moratto for the beautiful design. To my friends and family for their love and care.

Many thanks to Anna Van Valkenburg and everyone at Guernica Editions. And a special thank you to my publisher and editor Michael Mirolla for giving such a wonderful home to my novel.

About the Author

Guglielmo D'Izzia was born and raised in Sicily. He's an actor, a writer, and a gourmand. His artistic pursuits have led him to some of the greatest cities in the world: Rome, New York City, and eventually Toronto, where he now resides. He's a proud graduate of the creative writing program at the University of Toronto School of Continuing Studies. *The Transaction*, his debut novel, won the 2016 Marina Nemat Award. He's currently working on his second novel.

Printed in January 2020
by Gauvin Press,
Gatineau, Québec